Theodore Taylor

A SAILOR RETURNS

SCHOLASTIC ▌▌ SIGNATURE

AN IMPRINT OF SCHOLASTIC INC.

NEW YORK TORONTO LONDON AUCKLAND SYDNEY
MEXICO CITY NEW DELHI HONG KONG BUENOS AIRES

This book was originally published in hardcover by the Blue Sky Press in 2001.

ISBN 0-439-41771-6

12 11 10 9 8 7 6 5 4 3 2 1   2 3 4 5 6 7/0

Printed in the United States of America   40

First Scholastic club paperback printing, April 2002

Designed by Kathleen Westray

FOR ASHLEY TAYLOR,
WONDERFUL, BEAUTIFUL
GRANDDAUGHTER

Author's Note

I N 1978 I spent some time in quaint Mousehole, Cornwall, England. I became fascinated with the long history of the lifesaving station and the courageous seamen who manned the boats against unbelievable odds in storm-swept waters. The first rescue on record was in 1824. I decided to someday write about a Mousehole sailor. I chose Thomas "Chips" Pentreath.

I am deeply indebted to Doris Spriggs of Three Oaks Close, Middlesex, for her research assistance, particularly with Dartmoor Prison and the Cornish dialect.

— *Theodore Taylor*

1

T H E mail had arrived.

Brooklyn, New York
July 3, 1914

My dearest daughter:
I'm sure you'll be surprised to learn that I am still
alive. It has been almost thirty years since I last
saw you, just after your mother died, and I have much
to tell you. And now that I have at last found you,
after many letters to the postmasters at Cornwall's
Penzance, Newlyn, St. Ives, Lizard, Sennen, and
Coverack, as well as dear old Mousehole, I would like
very much to pay you a visit and exchange memories.
I am a retired ship's carpenter. . . .

Time was standing still, it seemed, to eleven-year-old Evan. A horsefly had somehow gotten into the house and zoomed around his mother's head. She batted at it without knowing what she'd done. She missed, and the horsefly plunged into the window screen and zoomed up again.

Though looking out of sorts at the moment, Jane Pentreath Bryant was a pretty lady, with flawless skin of ivory color and just as smooth, Cornish tinted. Her eyes were hazel. Her soft voice was slightly drawled from living in the South since childhood. Her teeth were dazzling. She was always pin-neat, in dress and manner.

"If he is my grandpa, he must be very old," said Evan.

She nodded, as if daydreaming. "Very old."

. . . I use a cane but get around very well and will not be a bother. Presently, I am living at the International Seaman's Last Harbor, address below.

With love, your father,

Thomas "Chips" Pentreath

Though she'd read it to Evan twice, she'd read it to herself silently, twice more.

He'd really said nothing about himself. What kind of man was he? Sailors didn't have good reputations. Could Evan be proud of him? Could she?

Ship's Carpenter Thomas "Chips" Pentreath of Mousehole, back from the dead.

"Well," she said, and Evan hung on those four letters as if chinning himself, expecting her to say something else. "Well, that's fine." Or, "Well, we'll have to think about this more."

Silence.

Finally, she said, still in a fog, "I haven't been to Mouzel, and that's the way it's pronounced, Mouzel, in thirty years. I was only three when your aunt Molly took me to America."

Evan well knew all that. He was fascinated that his mother had been born in such a place with such an odd name, near Land's End, in Cornwall, at the edge of the sea. He'd been told that long ago. He'd said that to many people: "Do you know that my mother was born in Mousehole, England?"

Where?

"'Exchange memories.' What memories?" she had said, with exasperation. "What memories, Evan? His? Mine?"

Evan shrugged, unable to ever remember his mother acting like this, so strangely.

"Well," she said again, taking a deep breath, shaking her head, sighing.

"Will you tell Grandpa that he can come and visit us?" Evander Bryant asked, hope plainly on his freckled face. His grandfather was suddenly a mystery man, already exciting.

"Please, Mama," he'd added quickly, already trying to imagine this old sailor, Thomas Pentreath, who wasn't supposed to be alive. Imagine kin from an odd place called Mousehole, in England, far across the sea. Imagine an old, old, jolly man, with merry eyes and deep laughter, who could talk about his adventures and China and Africa and South America, maybe the North Pole, maybe the South Seas, maybe Tahiti, about anything at all.

"Evan, this kind of thing happens all the time. Long-lost grandpas or uncles or cousins or sons or daughters, husbands, wives, suddenly reappear, years later. It happens all over the world every day, I have to think. I really do." Yesterday, she had *no* father. Today . . .

Standing there, in a blue and white apron, bulged around the middle, blackberry juice on her hands, Evan's mother looked as if all the ghosts in her ancient Cornish village had just clanked by. She shook her head slowly, stunned by the letter that had arrived moments before.

"Does that mean no?" Evan asked. "He can't come here?"

"No, that doesn't mean no," she answered vaguely.

The only sound in the kitchen that startling day came from the bubbling cast-iron cooker on the coal stove. Last year's empty jam jars were thumping up and down against the iron sides.

His mother stayed motionless, frowning, not sure of herself, cheeks reddened from the range heat, dark hair steamy damp.

Long ago, she'd told Evan that her father was lost at sea in the late 1800s. Gone forever without a trace. She read his letter again, aloud, not quite believing it.

Evan waited for her to make a sentence. It didn't come out.

Rubbing her chin, getting blackberry juice on it, she went out of the kitchen to the back stoop, sitting down in the sunshine by their black cat, Ponder, fanning herself with the Brooklyn envelope.

Evan's red setter, Woodrow, "Woody," named after the new president, Woodrow Wilson, was out in the backyard grass snapping at white moths.

His mother was still frowning.

"I remember your aunt Molly talking about my father. He was born in 1844 and was sort of a fishing scalawag, she said. Went into the lifeboat service as a very young man, performing heroic rescues at sea, and then sailed in the grain ships to Australia, big barks. He married my mother when he was once home from Perth. She was twenty. Sailors of those days sometimes just disappeared, lost at sea or winding up living in Shanghai."

A fishing scalawag? Evan wondered what that meant.

Woody got too close, and Ponder spit at him.

Shanghai was in China, Evan knew. Had his grandpa lived over there, riding in rickshaws?

Where else had his grandpa been the last thirty years? Had he been in a war?

Aunt Molly was dead, and so there was no one else alive to say anything, good or bad, about the mysterious Cornishman. "How did he find us?" That alone was a mystery.

She didn't answer.

Evan sat down beside his mother and stroked Ponder. "You don't seem excited."

"Evan, I don't know what to *seem*. I'm shocked. Truly shocked."

"What does scalawag mean?" He'd heard the word before but wasn't exactly sure what it meant.

"A ne'er-do-well. Someone who is a rascal or worse."

"A bad man? Grandpa is a bad man?"

"Oh, Evan, I have no idea what he's like. I don't even have an old photo of him. I have no idea what he looks like. He may be a very nice man, but he's a total stranger."

If ever a house needed excitement, it was theirs, Evan thought. He lived in the dullest house on the dullest street in town. It always seemed that way. A rascal might be fun.

She looked at him, making a helpless face. "I guess I'll let your father decide." Then she added, "Yes, I'm curious. I'd like to know what he's done all these years; why he never contacted me. But I won't have him here if your father objects. Why, oh why, didn't he write last year or the year before?"

Jane Bryant was almost nine months pregnant this midsummer. For reasons unknown she hadn't been able to provide a brother or sister to Evan, and now that she was thirty-three she didn't want anything, or *anybody*, to disturb that big bulge of baby curled behind her blue and white apron. Including her ghostly own father. A bronco belly kick reminded her of the near future.

"It took him a long time to find us, didn't it?" Evan asked.

Ignoring him, she talked into the blue, cloudless sky. "A week or so might be all right. But I know I'll feel awkward. All those years!"

"A week or so, after he comes all the way from Brooklyn?"

Drawing her eyes back from the sky, gazing at Evan, she said, "Brooklyn is a train ride, a day away."

To Evan, Brooklyn seemed as far as Mousehole.

The alarm clock went off in the kitchen. Jars all steamed and sterilized. Evan's mother rose up creakily, putting her hands on her hips and arching her back. "I guess it'll be all right for a few days."

A few days? Evan's heart fell. How about weeks? Months? Years? He needed someone to talk to. He had problems.

She went on inside to fill the mason jars and put a layer of paraffin over the sweet berry jam. With Buddy Jensen, Evan had helped pick three gallons in the tangles of bushes along the Deep Creek Canal. First berries of the season as big as his father's thumbs, shiny purple black.

Now hopeful that Grandpa would spend at least a week or more in the two-story white house on green-lawned Hoople Street, white picket fence in front, buggy barn and horse pasture in back, Evan hobbled across to where the Jensens lived, where Buddy lived. They were the same age, went to the same school, and did most of the same dull things during winter and summer. Red Woody tagged along. He was always faithful, always protective.

Evan announced importantly that his grandpa from Brooklyn, who had been a sailor to Australia and a lifeboat man, would soon arrive by train if his dad agreed.

Buddy looked up from the front steps of his house, which looked a lot like Evan's house. "I didn't think you had a grandfather on either side."

"Neither did we. He wasn't dead at sea after all."

"Can he take us fishing?" Buddy had a long face, and hair the color of ripe wheat. Evander had dark brown curly hair like his mother. He was an image of Jane Bryant, but she wasn't freckled. He had her warm smile and quiet voice.

"Oh, yes, he can take us fishing," said Evan. "He walks with a cane but gets around very well."

"Maybe he could take us on a boat down the river," said Buddy, whose real name was Vilhelm. Nobody called him that. Not even his Swedish parents. They regretted giving him that name. Buddy's daddy got seasick, even on a river, so he wouldn't take them fishing. Buddy was a true friend but skeptical of everything. His whole life was questions.

Evan nodded. "He can do that. He's a very big man and very strong, even though he's very old. My mother said he was a rascal."

Buddy said, "That's good."

2

"Do you remember that sailor who came back here a year ago after being away for a long time and chopped his whole family up with an ax?" Buddy Jensen said.

They were playing marbles on the hardscrabble barn floor, the color of mahogany. Woody, Toby, the black gelding, and the chickens looked on.

"I remember," Evan said. "He was from Churchland, not Portsmouth."

"He killed his mother and father and two sisters, then set fire to their farmhouse." Buddy liked to deal in awful things. Blood and bodies.

"I remember."

"He'd been gone from here twenty years. He'd smoked a lot of opium over in China, the paper said."

"What's that got to do with my grandfather?" Evan was frowning.

"Nothing, except that both of them were away for a long time."

Evan said, "The paper said that the sailor was insane from all that smoking. Well, he's in the crazy house up in Petersburg for the rest of his life. Nothing like my grandpa." He hoped.

"I wonder if your grandfather ever sailed with insane people."

"Probably. He's been everywhere around the world and had to run into crazy people."

"How do you know until you talk to him?"

"My aunt Molly said it. He's sailed on all the Seven Seas."

Buddy said, "Well, there happen to be a lot more than seven."

Evan often got frustrated with Buddy Jensen because he was a know-it-all. Yet he was often right. "I'm talking about the main ones."

He aimed his agate marble at Buddy's yellow glass

one in the ring's center circle and thumbed it four feet, making a direct hit. At least he was a better shooter than Buddy Jensen.

Buddy said, "Let's hope your grandpa doesn't come down here touched in the head."

Evan sat back angrily. "I don't want to hear any more from you about my grandpa."

Buddy stared back. "I'll make up my mind when I meet him."

They finished the game, and Buddy went home.

The overhead wooden fan in the dining room stirred the warm air, splatting it.

Evan sat quietly, listening, barely chewing. That was his habit around his father, answering when spoken to. He knew to swallow questions, not interrupt.

His father asked, suspiciously, "How did he find us?"

"Howard, I have no idea. None at all," said his mother.

"How would he know your married name?"

"I have no idea."

"He must have had help finding us."

That was a question Evan planned to ask. Definitely.

"Howard, I don't know."

"Evan, please pass the applesauce," his mother requested.

Evander, named after his father's father, now deceased, founder of Evander Bryant Shoes, on High Street, did so, sliding the glass bowl across the polished oak long table. He always sat quietly in the middle of the table, parents on both ends, like being in an adult sandwich. The menu tonight was breaded pork chops, black-eyed peas, a garden salad, and fresh strawberries with thick cream.

"Well, you've never had much good to say about your father. Isn't that the truth?"

Evan's mother laughed softly. "I've never had much to say about him, period. I've never known that much about him. I've told you what Molly told me. She loved her brother but said he was always a little wild and drank too much. Always a sailor under canvas. She didn't think he'd abandoned me purposely."

"Now we know he did abandon you, don't we? Don't we?"

"I guess he did. Now that we know he's alive, I guess he did abandon me."

Maybe he was washed up on some lonely island in the South Seas, living with the natives for a long time, Evan thought. Maybe he *couldn't* get in touch. Then a ship visited his island a few years ago and rescued him. He'd signed that letter "with love," hadn't he? Evan thought his father was already picking on his grandfather. Hadn't he truthfully said, "I have much to tell you . . ."? Evan crossed his fingers.

After a moment, Howard Bryant, forking a piece of pork chop into his mouth, said, "It's up to you, my dear. He's your father. I'll be polite, and I'll also look forward to hearing his tale about not writing you for thirty years. I frankly don't think much of sailors." Evan's father was as straitlaced as a paint yardstick. There were a lot of things he didn't think "much of."

Evan breathed a sigh of relief. Grandpa Pentreath could pay a visit.

After supper, Buddy Jensen came over and they caught lightning bugs in the front yard while Evan's parents sat in wooden rockers on the front porch. They put the bugs in a mason jar and then released them when it was totally dark.

Portsmouth, Virginia
July 10, 1914

Dear Father:
Yes, I was quite surprised to receive your letter, having grown up with the knowledge that you were lost at sea when I was very young. After thirty years, you must understand that it was a shock to learn that you are still alive. I'm still in shock.

I presume there are reasons why you did not try to find me until now. Your sister Molly passed away five years ago thinking that you were dead. Doubtless you will tell me those reasons during your visit.

You'll be glad to learn, I'm sure, that you have a fine grandson, Evander, eleven years old, whose letter is enclosed, and that I am pregnant again, finally. My husband, Howard, and I are hoping for a girl. Another grandchild for you.

You will be most welcome at our house, and we look forward to seeing you soon. Please let me know the date and time of your arrival. Evan and I will meet the train.

Sincerely,
Jane

Dear Grandfather:
I am so glad that you are coming to see us. I can't wait. I have not had a grandfather since I was three, and I don't remember him. His name was Evander, like mine. I need a grandpa. I hope you like to fish. My father never has time to do that, working at his store six days a week. He sings in the choir on Sundays, morning and evening.

Love,
Evan

Evan went to bed thinking about his grandfather's visit.

———

In the morning, Howard Bryant went along to Evander Bryant Shoes. For as long as Evan could remember, his father had worn a bow tie to work, always blue in the summer and red in the winter, and a slightly starched white shirt and gray pants. In the summer, he wore a shiny alpaca jacket, the color of ripe figs, and a straw skimmer. Of medium height and build, with thinning hair, he looked the same every single weekday. On summer Sundays for church, he wore a white linen coat. He was lead tenor in the choir and looked very wholesome in his rimless glasses. He was a member of the Moonyah Fellowship Club.

He walked the five blocks to the High Street trolley, carrying the alpaca jacket in his right arm so it wouldn't get sweaty. He was as regular as the town clock on High Street. When Deacon Howard Bryant passed, all was well. When Deacon Howard Bryant carried an umbrella, everyone knew it was going to rain. It usually did.

Though Howard was ten years older than she was, Jane Pentreath, former secretary at an insurance company, at eight dollars a week, married him

3

"MAMA said that disappeared people, brothers and sisters, fathers and mothers, show up all the time. So there's nothing strange about my grandfather showing up thirty years after he disappeared."

Buddy Jensen said, "I still think it's strange. He was hiding somewhere, I'll bet."

"Hiding from who?" Evan asked.

Buddy shrugged, then said, "Police."

Evan said, "You have a bad mouth."

Buddy shrugged again.

"I went to the library yesterday to find out about grain ships and Mousehole. Mrs. Roberts helped me with the square-riggers, the sailing ships to Australia, but we couldn't even find Mousehole on the Cornwall map. I guess it's too little." Evan often checked books out of the library.

"That's a crazy name for a village," Buddy said.

"My grandpa will tell us all about it once he gets here. I've been thinking about him night and day."

"When's he coming?"

"In two days. His sister, Molly, told my mother he was six feet four, and weighed two hundred fifty pounds. He's got steel in his arms for muscles." Molly hadn't said that. Evan now and then exaggerated.

"That's a very big man, Evan," Buddy said.

They were out by the barn, having hosed down the buggy, a regular chore for Evan on Saturdays. He earned his weekly dime allowance taking care of Toby, the buggy, and the chickens. The Bryants always took the buggy to church, which was three miles away.

"He's also tattooed, like all sailors." That was a pure guess, and hope. "On his arms and chest." And he'd have a great white beard.

"Does he speak English?" Buddy asked.

"Of course, he does. Cornwall is in England. I thought last night about something else. You know I want to build a rowboat so we can fish out of it. Who better to help me build that boat than my grandpa? Then we go out in it. I think it should have three seats in it and be twelve feet long. He's a retired ship's carpenter, you know. Chips is his nickname, like wood chips."

Buddy said, "I'll help build it, but I still wonder where he was all those thirty years."

"I think I know," Evan said. "He was shipwrecked in the South Seas and floated on a mast all the way to Tahiti, where the natives pulled him ashore. He fell in love with a beautiful girl, and they had a baby. The baby died, then she died, and he was rescued when a ship full of missionaries came there." The name "Tahiti" fascinated him.

Buddy said, "Why didn't he get in touch with your mother after the missionaries rescued him?"

Evan admitted he didn't know. He hobbled over to turn the water off.

Evan had a clubfoot, a *talipes valgus,* his right one; the foot rotated and turned outward. He was born that way, the doctor saying that he had adopted an abnormal position in the womb. The doctor tried to manipulate his foot the day after he was born, wrench it straight, but it didn't work. His mother felt guilty about it, he knew.

Evan couldn't run. When he tried, he looked like he was in a potato sack race. He walked on his heel, his toes turned upward. He could jump but often fell down. His father had a special shoe made for the clubfoot, a clumpish ugly thing. Though he didn't often complain, he envied boys who had two good feet. Sometimes the other kids made fun of him, calling him "big foot" or "shoe boy."

Normally there was no pain in his foot, but he hated to look at it, and his mother took oversized socks and tailored them for the odd-shaped thing at the bottom of his right leg. He never went barefoot in public. He never went to the town swimming pool for that reason.

Buddy helped him wipe off the buggy seat, saying, "Why did both that Tahiti girl and her baby die?"

"I don't know," Evan answered. "I'll ask him."

Then they hosed down and groomed Toby, so he would look nice in the churchyard the next day. Evan's father prided himself on having both the buggy and the horse look good alongside the transportation of other worshipers.

Evan went to Sunday School in the morning, attended the regular church services, and then they went back for Vespers Sunday evening after their usual fried chicken dinner with mashed potatoes and green peas, watermelon or ice cream in the summer.

Evan thought they overdid it on Sundays. He sometimes had a stomachache during Vespers. But his father sang tenor, sometimes solo, wishing the congregation could applaud.

Evan had had dreams about his father. Once, his father's face had turned into the devil's head. Another dream he had, his father was whipping Toby, and Evan hobbled out to stop him. There had been other dreams, his father often angry.

"After those natives of Tahiti rescued him, how did he live?" Buddy Jensen wanted to know.

"They taught him how to build a hut out of dried palm fronds. You've seen those huts in that geography magazine."

"The one that has those half-naked native women in it?"

"That's the one."

They were in Buddy's tree house.

"All right, what did he eat?"

"He ate coconut meat and oranges, and they taught him how to make a spear so he could fish out on the reefs."

"It sounds to me like he enjoyed himself on Tahiti."

"He must have," Evan said.

"All right, how did he meet his wife?"

Evan thought a while. "She was the chief's daughter, a princess, and didn't think any of the native men were good enough for her. So here comes this big sailor out of the water, and she takes one look at my grandpa and decides he will be her husband. He had no choice. And that is all right since my Mousehole grandmother was dead."

Buddy said, "I guess."

"She had long dark hair and beautiful dark skin. She wore coral beads around her neck and wore grass skirts."

"Wouldn't they itch?"

"I don't know."

"Did she wear a top?"

Evan said, "I don't know."

"Could she dance?"

"Yes. She was a good dancer."

"Did the chief agree to her marrying your grandfather?"

"He thought it was fine, and they had a huge wedding service with the high priest of Tahiti conducting it. They had a great feast that lasted all night, with hogs roasted in a pit and fruits you've never heard of. My grandfather wore a headband of tiny white orchids, and he danced, too. The drums went until dawn."

"How about their honeymoon?"

"They went off in an outrigger canoe, just the two of them, to an uninhabited island and spent a month there, living off the land."

"Evan, why did your grandfather ever leave Tahiti?"

"Well, he was sad after the baby died, and then the princess died, and along came the missionaries."

4

"I didn't sleep much last night. Grandpa's coming tomorrow. I figured out why he's coming."

"Why?" Buddy Jensen asked.

"Well, he wants to see his family, but beyond that, he wants to tell us about hidden treasure."

"Where is it hidden?"

"On Deadman's Cay."

"Where is that?"

"An island in the Great Bahama Banks, off Florida."

"Where did you hear about all that?"

"That same geography magazine that told about Tahiti and had those pictures of half-nude women. I looked at it this morning."

"How would he know about any hidden treasure?"

"He fell overboard when his ship was passing Deadman's Cay, and he swam ashore. The magazine said that the island was used by pirates long ago. He was on there two or three days when he saw something shining, half-buried in the sand. It was a gold bar."

"Evan, don't you think a lot of other people searched that island if they thought pirates had been there?"

"My grandpa swam ashore not long after a hurricane passed by. It disturbed the sand."

"So what's he going to do? Tell you where to look for the gold bars?"

"He's been thinking how to pay my mother for those thirty years he didn't get in touch with her."

"Evan, you're telling me all these stories about your grandfather to make me believe he is something special. You don't even know that he ever sailed anything more than a ferry boat."

"Isn't he living in that International Seaman's Last Harbor in Brooklyn?"

"He could have lied to them to get room and board. Sailors and fishermen are the worst liars on earth."

Buddy's mother said, "Stop it, you boys."

Evan got up and slammed the Jensens' kitchen door and hobbled home, mumbling to himself.

Evan stood on the platform with his mother, awaiting the arrival of his grandfather. He had not been this excited since Woody was allowed to join the family the previous year as a red ball of puppy. His father didn't care too much for dogs. Woody couldn't enter the house. He slept in the barn with Toby and the chickens. Ponder slept in the house.

Then, far off, a whistle blew at a crossing, and soon the tracks began to vibrate. Evan asked nervously, "What do I say to him?"

His mother, tense and tight lipped herself, said, "I'm the last person on earth to ask. Say hello."

Then the train came into sight, whistling again, brass bell beginning to ring. Shoving out cones of steam on either side, the engine soon led the dark green cars by the platform. Evan stared at the faces in the windows as though he might instantly know Thomas Pentreath.

Passengers began to alight, and from the next car to the last emerged an old man in a shapeless tweed jacket, black cap on his head, cane in his right hand, a dingy canvas bag in his left hand. He looked as if he might vanish into the engine's wind-twisted coal smoke. He had the face of a hairless monkey.

Jane Bryant said, "I think that may be my father."

Evan said, with huge disappointment, "But he's so small," and followed his mother. He'd truly expected a giant of a man in sailor pants with huge muscles, walking with a sailor's roll, a man he'd invented. This one had a limp Evan noticed immediately.

They began walking toward the stranger, and a few steps later they came face-to-face with Thomas Pentreath. He spoke first, a cautious smile making up over the wrinkles. "Jane Bryant?"

Evan's mother smiled back shyly. "Father?"

Then he said, "Daughter?" Tears brimmed.

She nodded and held out her hand. Evan thought she didn't look at all like her father.

"Oh, my," he said. "And this is Evander?"

Despite the size problem, Evan grinned and threw

his arms around his grandfather. He was what Evan had wanted for a long time, someone in his own house to talk to besides his mother.

Tom Pentreath took a deep, deep breath. "Never did I think this would happen."

"Neither did I," Evan's mother said. Evan agreed.

Tom took two steps backward. "Let me look at both of you. You are so pretty, Daughter. And you are so handsome, Grandson." The monkey face was now beaming.

Evan beamed back.

It was one of those moments when no one quite knew what else to say. "How was your trip down?" Jane asked.

"Oh, very well. I've always liked trains but haven't traveled on many."

"Evan brought the buggy. It's much too far to walk to our house."

The first automobile had come to Portsmouth in 1902. There were now twelve horseless carriages: two Model T Fords owned by the police, an Oldsmobile, a Locomobile, a Packard, a Metz, a Simplex, a Stutz, a

Pierce-Arrow, and several more. Evan's father was saving for a Model T.

So they went to the hitching rail near the station where many buggies and horses were lined up, and they were soon on their way to Hoople Street. Evan proudly held the reins. Tom sat on the back seat.

Evan didn't know how to explain to Buddy Jensen that Tom Pentreath was really a rooster, two feet higher than Evan was, not six feet four. He could say that his grandfather shrunk because of old age. Buddy would laugh. And he didn't look like he'd spent much time in Tahiti, much less married a princess. He wasn't at all handsome, but he was here.

Finally, Evan spoke. "I have a dog named Woody, after our new president."

"I've always liked dogs. I had two or three when I was a boy in Mouzel."

"You have to tell me about that village, Grandpa."

"Oh, I will, I will . . ."

Evan's mother asked, "How in the world did you find me?"

Evan thought, I'd like to know, too.

"It was actually quite simple, Daughter. There was an ad in the *New York Times* classified offering the services of the Mr. Look Agency. They trace lost persons. As you know, Pentreath is not a common name in this country. So they searched and found you, Jane Pentreath Bryant, of Mousehole, England, not a common name, either."

He didn't tell her he'd saved for three years to pay the fee. He'd done odd jobs — carpentry, emptied garbage, cleaned toilets, and the like.

They all three chatted back and forth as Toby clomped along. Reaching home, Woody greeting them, Ponder staring suspiciously at the newcomer. Jane said, "You'll have the room and bath upstairs, Father. Opposite my sewing room. Evan will show you."

"Anywhere at all," Tom said, still beaming.

At the top of the stairs, Evan said, "We already have something in common. Both of us limp."

Tom nodded. "I noticed, Evander."

"I have a clubfoot."

"And I broke an ankle long ago at sea. It was not set properly."

"We'll look funny walking beside each other."

"We'll walk proudly, Evander, and pay no attention to others; I never have."

"You can stay here forever," Evan said.

Tom laughed. "Forever is a long time."

"Grandpa, were you ever shipwrecked near an island, near one like Tahiti?"

"No. My only shipwreck was in the Java Sea."

"You must tell me about it."

"Oh, I will."

"Grandpa, did you ever fall overboard on the Great Bahama Banks and swim ashore to Deadman's Cay, which was a pirate island long ago?"

Tom laughed again. "No, Evander. I fell overboard several times, but never in the Bahamas."

Evan said, "I was hoping that had happened, so I could tell my best friend." He sounded disappointed.

"Evander, tell him I fell overboard around the world but not in the Bahamas."

"You can call me Evan, you know."

"I prefer to call you Evander. It's such a nice English name." His delft blue eyes were warm and full of love.

"Whatever," Evan said. It already seemed he'd known his grandfather for years.

They went on into the room, and Tom said, "My!" It was painted yellow, neat and clean, with taffeta curtains and a multicolored crocheted rug by the bed. "My," Tom repeated. "Do you know that this is the first private home I've been in since leaving Mouzel?"

"Really?" That sounded impossible. Never a real home, always ships.

Tom had no close friends at ISLH, a four-story brick building occupied solely by lonesome, talkative retired seamen, and supported by the Maritime Episcopal Church. There was only one person residing in the building with whom he'd ever sailed, and Captain Scowcroft, as tough and demanding today as he was when he skippered the four-masted grain ships to Australia, wasn't much of a friend at that.

What should he tell the Bryants about himself? Truthfully, he'd been a rounder, a gutter drunk with a bad temper. He'd fought big men in his time, though a bantamweight, and lost to them. He counterpunched. A few he'd knocked out. Bar brawls. He'd had girls in a lot of ports around the world.

"Cap'n, my last chance on earth to see my daughter. But should I tell her the truth about what happened on the *Hartlepool*? About the killing? About Dartmoor? I have a fine grandson, Evander, and don't want him to think badly of me."

"Tell her the truth, all of it! Tell the boy the truth, all of it!" said Scowcroft, those frozen gray eyes growing in intensity. "Yes, tell them you are a killer." The captain seemed to enjoy using that word.

But he was a changed man now, had been since terrible Dartmoor Prison. Should he take Cap'n Scowcroft's advice and tell them about that single time? Plead for his daughter's forgiveness, ask Evander to understand that he was not the same man of a quarter century ago? Would they understand? Would they believe him?

Would his daughter's husband, knowing the kind of man he'd been, order him to leave their house as a matter of safety? Would the husband realize he'd changed? Would Jane and Evander be afraid of him? Once a killer, always a killer, the saying went. It wasn't true, in his case.

What should he especially tell Evander? What would the boy want to hear? Except for the time in prison, the memories were all about the sea, fourteen different ships, the last two coal-burners; maybe a hundred different ports. Most boys liked to hear about adventure.

There was that long period in the South Seas, under sail. There had been gales and typhoons; there'd been piracy in the Philippines; there'd been all kinds of shipmates, from the dangerous, even murderous, to the pitiful.

Looking back, he really hadn't accomplished any-thing at all; he was a penniless failure. He had wasted his entire life. At the end of his stay in Portsmouth that's what he'd truthfully tell Evander. He'd talk about his sea experiences except for Ozzie O'Brien and the Hartlepool, the half-minute violence that had cost him eleven years in Dartmoor Prison. He'd tell Evander never to become a sailor.

Evan said, "I noticed your cane. That's a dragon's head on the handle, isn't it?"

Tom nodded. "I carved it out of a piece of birch."

"You carve?"

"Many sailors do it to pass time in good weather, especially becalmed. Not a breath of wind."

5

E V A N almost floated downstairs and said to his mother, in the kitchen, "Isn't he wonderful?"

Jane nodded, but the look on her face said, "Let's wait a while." Her father was, after all, a total and complete stranger. There had to be dark periods in his life. What were they?

Evan went on outside to take care of Toby, unhitch him, lead him back into the barnyard, make sure he had plenty of water. The day was hot.

When he went back into the kitchen, his grandpa was there. He had a gift for each of them. A small bottle of perfume for his mother, a small hand-carved ship's model for Evan. He'd taken off his jacket and wore wide blue suspenders over his blue denim shirt.

Except for his boots, Evan didn't think he looked much like a sailor. He did not have a beard.

His mother said, "We're having our special Sunday meal for supper this evening. I want you two to make some ice cream."

Ice was delivered twice a week by horse wagon, a pair of fifty-pound blocks during the summer. If extra ice was needed, Evan would take Toby to the ice-house on Tidewater Street.

"I've never done that, made ice cream," said Tom.

Evan said, "It's easy. We'll do it about four o'clock, and let it sit until supper under a blanket." He'd had charge of the freezer crank since he was seven or eight.

His mother said, "I bought some nice, fresh strawberries yesterday."

Evan finally felt as if he had a real family with his grandfather there. But he worried about his father, who would close the shoe store promptly at five-thirty and take the trolley home. How would he treat Grandpa? Not very well, Evan predicted.

Evan said, "We take a couple of big pieces of ice

and pound them into bits inside a towel with a mallet. Then we stick the ice into the wood pail, and sprinkle some rock salt on it. Mama makes the cream mixture, then we dump it into the galvanized container, close it up, and crank. I'll show you."

Tom said, "Homemade ice cream," as if it was a miracle.

"Let me show you around," said Evan, and Tom followed him outside into the barn, which had a stall for Toby, a hayloft, and chicken coops. His father had a tool bench in there but seldom had time to fix anything. He wouldn't work on the Sabbath, he'd just go to church and read the papers and nap. Sunday was always a disaster for Evan. Everyone on Hoople Street took naps.

Tom commented, "Those are very good tools."

"They belonged to my other grandfather, who died when I was small."

Evan took him across the pasture to the tree-hung creek bank. The water was muddy brown. "I hope you'll help me build a rowboat." Woody trotted beside them.

"I'm not sure I'll be around that long."

"I want you here for the rest of my life," Evan said emphatically.

"I just came for a visit," Tom answered. *He would not burden this nice family.*

"Grandpa, did you ever go to school?"

"Of course I did. Like most other village boys I dropped out when I was fourteen to work on the fishing boats. But I was a good student. Mathematics was difficult for me, but I read and wrote very well."

"That is just like me. I hate math."

They sat down outside the barn.

"It's very important to your education."

"Grandpa, will you speak Cornish for me? My friend, Buddy Jensen, had never heard of Cornwall."

"Cornish? Oh, my. Oh, my. It was already fading out when I was a boy in that wee village. Did not Aunt Molly speak some Cornish to you?"

"I was six when she died. She was very sick with cancer her last two years."

Tom's face fell. "I didn't know. I'm so sorry for her."

To those who spoke the King's English, the people

of Cornwall were considered "foreigners," generally stupid people who spoke a dialect that only their pigs understood, Tom told Evan. "You would say, 'Are you going to do it?' in good King's English, and I would say in Cornish, 'Are ee gwain to do it, or aren't ee?' I remember cleaning out the chilter, which was the shelter, or cowshed; the pigs' crow was the sty."

Tom stopped and thought a while. "Mother was mawthur. Let's see now. One of my early jobs was to carry the cluckers. That meant removing the broody hens from the nests. And, oh yes, young pullets were known in West Cornwall as mabyers, and when the eggs were hatching we said they were beelin, and a yewel was a dung fork."

Tom stopped again and said, "I have to think." After a moment, he said, "The dialect word most used was 'scat.' I remember getting scats 'cross me mud-dick, which was the back of my head."

"Muddick?" Evan repeated and laughed.

"I'll tell you all the Cornish names for just plain stupid — aisy gwains, doodas, droozenheads, knaw gwain nowheers, buccagwiddens, goostrumnoodles cobbas, and doughys. . . ."

"Grandpa, you have to teach me Cornish by the time school starts."

Tom said, "Oh, my. I have a lot of thinking to do."

He yawned and said he thought he should take a little nap.

6

"WHERE is he?" Buddy Jensen asked.

"He's upstairs taking a nap," Evan replied.

"When will he wake up?"

"How do I know? He said a 'little nap.'"

"Tell me what he looks like."

"He has clipped white hair and blue eyes. Plenty of wrinkles."

"And he's six feet four and weighs two hundred fifty pounds?"

It was a question Evan dreaded. "Aunt Molly must have been having a glass of ale when she said that." Blame it on Aunt Molly.

"How tall is he?"

"About two feet taller than we are."

Buddy shook his head. "Are you sure he's even a sailor?"

"I'm sure of that."

"Has he told you any sea stories?"

"Buddy, we got him off the train and brought him straight here. He didn't have time to tell us any sea stories. But he did talk to me in Cornish."

"Tell me a word."

"Muddick. It means the back of your head."

Buddy poofed out a disgusted breath. He'd expected a giant of a man. "Does he have tattoos?"

"He's wearing a long-sleeve shirt."

"My daddy tries to hide his, too. He was a private in the Spanish-American War. Did you ask him about Tahiti?"

"Yes. He was shipwrecked in the Java Sea."

"Is that near Tahiti?"

"I don't think so."

Buddy said, "Nothing that you told me about him is true. Nothing."

Just then, there was a creaking of stairs, and Evan said, "That's him."

They hurried out of the front room where the

"Grandpa Watch" was taking place just as the man from Mousehole took his final downward step.

Evan said, "Grandfather, I'd like you to meet my best friend, Buddy Jensen. He lives just up the street."

Buddy's eyes narrowed as Tom extended his hand.

Buddy's first words were, "When can we go fishing?"

Tom obviously felt uncomfortable at the supper table under the stern gaze of his daughter's husband. Howard Bryant was not very cordial when they met shortly after he arrived home. He was polite but aloof, to Evan's dismay.

At the dinner table, it wasn't long before Mr. Bryant asked, matter-of-factly, "Where have you been all these thirty years since you last saw your daughter?"

These fine, wholesome members of this family, his only family, would not understand the circumstances, Tom thought. He would try to be as honest as he could, try to talk his way around the dark history.

"I was at sea a lot of the time. As you know, a sailor

can be away for years. A ship can run between two ports in the Far East on many voyages."

Evan felt sorry for his grandfather.

"When did you last visit that village you call Mouzel?"

"About three years after Molly took Jane to America."

"And she didn't leave you a message?"

Evan wished his father would shut up.

"She'd sold the cottage, and it was occupied by people I didn't know. They hadn't received any word from her since she sailed out of London."

"That's strange," Mr. Bryant said. "Very strange."

That's what Buddy Jensen had said, Evan thought.

"Unfortunate more than strange," Tom said.

His grandfather's face was taut.

"You made no attempt to ask others in the village if they'd had any word. Your sister had friends there, Molly told me."

"Yes, she did."

"You abandoned your daughter, didn't you, Pentreath?" Mr. Bryant accused.

Evan felt terrible.

Jane said, "Why don't we finish dinner and then talk on the porch?"

"Your father hasn't answered my question."

"I didn't abandon her on purpose, sir. The bark that I was on simply didn't return to England for three years. All I knew, sir, was that Molly had taken my daughter to America. America is a very big country."

"Molly said she'd addressed several letters to you in care of the post office in Mousehole."

"Letters were first sent to Penzance, a village not far away, then transferred to Mouzel. I checked both Penzance and Mouzel for any letters that might be addressed to me. There were none. They might have been thrown away due to time."

"Your reasons are not very satisfying to me, Pentreath."

"I wish you'd call me Tom."

Evan wanted to run outside.

His mother said, "Howard, what difference does it make now? I have no ill feelings. We're reunited."

"Were you and Molly on good terms when you last saw her?"

"We argued occasionally." *He wanted to tell them*

but feared he'd be asked to leave tonight. Unpaid in the lifeboat service, he was running with that rough Mouzel crowd of young men. They rowed out to sea to save poor souls when ships were foundering. They drank hard and fought hard, and he manned his oar with the biggest of them. He was as tough and wiry as an oak limb.

At the age of twenty-two, already a widower, he was proud of his lifesaving role, but Molly wanted him safe onshore to raise his daughter. Yes, they argued. He was earning his uncertain living as a pilchard, cod, and mackerel fisher.

"It seems to me, Pentreath," Mr. Bryant said, "that the greatest priority in your life would have been to find little Jane by any means."

Evan swallowed hard, shaking his head.

"I agree," Tom said, looking over at his daughter, his face white and tense.

"Under the circumstances, Pentreath, I would think a week here would be plenty of time to visit your daughter and your grandson."

Tom nodded. *He was getting what he deserved.*

Evan's face was pale as his father rose from the table and marched out to the front porch. Just a week? He fought back tears.

"I should have found you," Tom admitted to Jane.

"We all make mistakes, and I forgive you," his daughter said, making Evan feel a little better.

Tom said, "Excuse me," and went out to the front porch, where Mr. Bryant was occupying a rocker. He said, "The door to my room is sticking. May I have permission to fix it? I'm a good carpenter."

"Suit yourself, but don't break any of my tools." Howard began rocking.

Evan heard the conversation from just inside the front door and made up his mind to defend his grandfather at every opportunity.

7

"MAMA, why can't Grandpa stay more than a week?" Evan asked. He'd tossed and turned all night.

"He can." Jane Bryant wasn't afraid of her husband, but he was so used to having his way. "I'll talk to him in a day or two."

Howard Bryant was a selfish man, she knew, and she knew he was too old, at forty-three, to change very much. Yet he was a good man and took good care of them.

"Grandpa may not want to stay longer than several weeks," she said, pushing the carpet sweeper in the living parlor. The baby's kicks were now around the clock.

"Can't we let Grandpa decide?" Evan said.

Tom entered the room after putting the carpenter's plane away in the barn. Evan had watched him fix the door.

"Evander, would you know where we might find some pigeons? And, Jane, might I have a little stale bread to feed them? I always do it every day in Brooklyn. It's an important part of my life."

Evan said, "There are always a lot of pigeons around the Confederate Monument. That's just off High Street. Can I come with you?"

"You'll have to. I don't know my way around."

"We'll take the trolley."

For more than three years, the usual day for Tom Pentreath was to arise, dress himself in a rather shabby coat and tie, and have a bun and strong breakfast tea in the Commons Room of the rest home. This was followed by a short, brisk walk, weather permitting, wool cap on his head. Then it was off to feed the beloved pigeons on a Brooklyn Heights park bench and look at ship traffic in and out of New York, ferries scurrying around, and finally end up in the library. He read books far into the night.

Evan's mother said, "As long as you're going, make a savings deposit for me. I'll give you an envelope."

They limped up Hoople Street toward High, Evan pointing out where Buddy Jensen lived and where Mr. Faircloth, the richest man in Portsmouth, lived. "He owns the biggest bank and has the most expensive automobile in town, a Stutz."

Tom said, "My, what a wonderful house."

"It was the first one on the block. With those big white columns, they call it a colonial. It has ten rooms. Mr. Faircloth's wife died several years ago, so he has a housekeeper and a cook. He also owns a racehorse."

"A very rich man, eh?"

"Some people don't like him. They say he's stingy and hard to work for."

"The more money you have, the more you want," Tom said.

"We have to go to his bank on High Street," Evan said.

They got on the trolley.

"Grandpa, tell me about Mousehole, please."

"It's such a wee village, so very old. . . ."

"How did it get that funny name? Mama doesn't know. Did a mouse go down a hole?"

"No one knows. It comes from an old Cornish name, Moeshayle, and in English, it is the village of Mouzel in Paul Parish in the Deanery and West Division of the Hundred of Penwith on the western shore of Mount's Bay, with its rough seas and beaten rocks and small coves. We know there was a market there in 1292, and Spanish soldiers with pikes and swords burned it to the ground on July 23, 1595. . . ."

"Oh, I'd like to go there. Will you take me, Grandpa?"

The trolley bucketed along as Tom thought how to answer Evander. He didn't want to admit he had no money after living all these years. Even if he had, he doubted Mr. Bryant or Jane would entrust him with Evander on the long voyage to England.

"There's nothing in the world that I'd like to do more than that, take you to my village, show you where I played as a boy and went to school and fished as a young man and went on sea rescues. . . ."

"Well, why can't we go?"

"You have your school and your family, Woody and Ponder and Toby . . ."

"Can't we think about it, and go when I'm all through school?"

"We can think about it, surely."

But Tom, deep down, knew that his days were numbered, as Captain Scowcroft had reminded him; knew that sometime the chest pains would become so severe that he'd no longer survive them. He took nitroglycerin pills three times a day.

They got off the trolley at the Court Street stop and walked a half block to Portsmouth Bank. Evan pointed to a dignified man with silver-gray hair. He was large, immaculately dressed. "That's Mr. Faircloth. I showed you his house on Hoople."

Tom nodded as Evan went up to a cashier's cage with the deposit envelope.

Then Evan led the way back to the foot of the Confederate Monument, which towered about forty feet above the ground, a lot of grayish pigeons perched on it or pecking around the base.

"Have you done this a long time, fed the pigeons?"

"A very long time, Evander, in many places."

How he'd like to tell Evander about Dartmoor Prison and the wonderful pigeons there, how they saved his life just by being friends. Yes, he should write that short history of his life to be read by his grandson after his final voyage and before they enclosed him in a weighted canvas shroud and buried him at sea.

More than ever, he would tell Evander never to follow in his footsteps, never be a drinker or fighter, never murder or be in prison. He would tell Evander to become a doctor or a lawyer, not a rootless sailor. He would tell Evander to have a loving family.

He began to talk to the pigeons.

"Do they understand you?"

"Yes, the moment I sat down here they knew I was friendly and would feed them."

Soon, there were dozens around his feet. "No matter whether it's London or Hong Kong, pigeons all speak somewhat the same, that hollow cooing."

"Are there pigeons everywhere around the world?"

Tom nodded. "Everywhere except the lands of snow and ice. It's a big family, Evander, including all the doves. The pigeons of New Guinea are as large as hen turkeys. There are blue pigeons in the Comoro Islands, and pink-breasted pigeons in the Philippines, green-winged pigeons in the Orient; rock doves, like these, everywhere."

"You'll have to tell me about all the islands you've been to, Grandpa."

"That's a lot, but I will tell you."

Tom finished the bag of stale bread and said, "Now, what shall we do?"

"Let's go to the Issac Fass Fishing Dock. It's only about six blocks from here. Buddy Jensen and I sometimes sneak away from home and go there to sit on a piling and watch the boats unload. Don't tell anyone, especially my father."

"Would he object?"

"I'm supposed to stay in the neighborhood."

"I won't tell," Tom promised.

When they reached the dock, Evan said, "I just sit here and watch the fishermen, knowing that someday I'll be like them." He often ignored his clubfoot when thinking of the future. Maybe he could be a ship's cook?

"It's a hard life," said Tom. "A very hard life."

"I've only been fishing three times, with Buddy Jensen. A neighbor took us, but then he died last year."

"I'll take you both," Tom promised.

"And will you help me build that rowboat?"

Tom said he would, wondering where he'd get the money to do that. He did have the cash to buy them each a nickel hot dog before going home. He had eleven dollars to spend in Portsmouth, plus change.

F O U R boats, back from the Atlantic, were tied up, and the fish were being shoveled into big wire-net baskets that were dumped into carts on the dock, then iced.

"Tell me why you quit fishing," Evan said.

"I didn't own a boat. I crewed, sharing whatever we sold. Sometimes we'd make money, sometimes none. The mackerel, pilchard, and herring would just disappear, and the salting cellars would be empty. A difficult life, Evander. You could lose all your nets in a sudden storm. Now and then I'd smuggle tobacco and perfume from Dutch ships offshore and sell them to Cornwall merchants, avoiding the hated British import tax. Wasn't legal, of course, but anything to make a little money. That's a secret, between us, the smuggling. Your mother was a baby then."

"Last night you started to tell me about the fishermen's superstitions."

Tom nodded, remembering back a half century.

"All of us were afraid of drowning. My own father drowned. We wouldn't walk along the shore at night where boats had been wrecked on the rocks for fear of running into the souls of dead men, particularly before incoming storms. The Cornish coast is one of the most treacherous in the world. Many fishermen, including me, swore we could hear the voices of the dead calling out their own names and the boats they died with. A voice from the sea would shout, 'The hour is come.' Repeat it three times. Then a black figure would appear at the top of the rocky cliffs and rush down into the water, sinking beneath the surface."

"I want to hear all those stories," said Evan.

On the trolley going home: "Picture Mount's Bay, a big body of water between Land's End and Lizard Point in Cornwall, and a terrible northeast storm comes rolling in between France and the English

Channel. The schooner *Carrie Goodworthy* is soon demasted and helpless in the raging sea. We manned a boat and rowed out to her, taking off eight crewmen, one by one, in ten-foot waves. Twice we almost foundered. Two men broke their arms. . . ."

"He is the smartest man in the world and knows more about fishing and pigeons than anyone. There's a pigeon in New Guinney as big as a turkey hen. . . ."

"Come on, Evan. A pigeon as big as a turkey?" said Buddy Jensen. "He's making that up."

"I don't think so. He won a silver medal when he was twenty-two for a sea rescue. There was this schooner caught in a terrible storm, and the boat from Mousehole went out to save the crew members. They broke seven oars but had a spare set. Grandpa rowed on five more rescues before he sailed for Australia."

"Where is he now?"

"He takes a nap every afternoon from three to five. Mama once said that Aunt Molly knew he was born in 1844."

"That makes him seventy," Buddy said, after a pause to count. "That's why he needs to take a nap."

"But he can live until he's ninety. I just hope he stays here. I think Mama will let him, but I don't think my father will. We're going to take a trip to England as soon as I get out of high school. He'll show me around, take me to Mouzel."

They were in Buddy's bedroom. He'd gotten an envelope of canceled foreign stamps in the morning mail. The stamps were spread over Buddy's bed.

"My living grandpa is a tobacco farmer near Richmond. He doesn't even want to see New York City."

"He's going to teach me how to speak Cornish, and I'll teach you."

Tom had awakened from his nap, put his boots on, splashed water on his face, and was now down in the kitchen, where his daughter was preparing supper. Most nights in the summer there was cold potato salad, chicken salad, carrot salad, beet salad, macaroni, sliced meat, fruit, and cake.

He sat on the high kitchen stool, pug face perplexed, and said, "Jane, this morning while we were at the fish docks, Evander asked me if I'd help him build a rowboat. Of course I will, but I do have a problem. I would love to pay for the wood that we'll need but I honestly don't have all the money." Ponder wove around his ankles.

"How much do you think it will cost?"

"I'll figure it up, but I guess by the time we count in oars and oarlocks and an anchor and rope, maybe thirty dollars."

Jane thought for a moment. "I have my own bank account, money saved up from what Howard gives me for household expenses. I shop for bargains."

"There'll be paint and caulking, brass screws. I forgot about them."

"When do you want to start?"

"Whenever Evander is ready."

Jane laughed. "That would be yesterday. He began talking about it the day we knew you'd be coming. But could you take Evan and Buddy fishing before you do the boat? Howard has never taken him, although Evan has begged him."

The more Tom learned about her husband, the less he liked him. If he only had a week here, two at most, each day with the boy was precious.

"I'll pack a lunch for the three of you when you decide to go," his daughter said. Then she looked at
him intently. "I'm so pleased you're here, Father."

*He nodded a thanks. Words couldn't express how he
felt. Why, oh why, hadn't he tried to do this ten years
ago, be with family? Even now, after sailing all those
years, wasn't he still gazing at the passing ships going
in and out of New York, ready to pack his seabag? Old
fool.*

"Tell me about the South Seas." Evan was in bed.
*In to say good night, Tom looked down at his
grandson. Here was a boy who'd never seen a real
palm tree or watched a tropic sunset. Only sailors like
himself or wanderers or artists and the rich had been
to the South Seas by this year of 1914. His memories
of the islands were treasured and easy to share.*

"Well, palm trees flutter and wave in the warm
breeze; natives have huts of bamboo and thatch, pan-
danus mats often beneath them as beds; beaches the
color of pearls shine in the moonlight; white terns fly
low over surf, crying out in joy; tall herons wade at
the shallow edge of the sea; white water breaks over

the reefs just offshore; clouds of all colors drift over the islands, driven by the trade winds; outrigger canoes come out at dawn and return at sunset with their catches. There is always peace and quiet.

"You'll never see fog, and the moon and stars seem to touch the palms. The pointers of the Big Dipper as it swings around in the heavens aim toward the North Star, which is always below the horizon. I can't really describe the sunsets, Evander. Sometimes the whole sky is laced with streamers of crimson, tinting the sea and beaches, bands of deep blue stretching across the horizon. . . ." *He'd been told he could be poetic by more than one sweetheart.*

"Please take me out there, Grandpa." Tahiti was always beckoning. He'd read all about it.

Oh, that I could, Tom wished. "We'll see."

Then he said good night and went slowly up the stairs, realizing he hadn't had any chest pains since arriving at his daughter's house. He made certain he took his TNT pills three times a day.

9

In the fresh, sunny morning, after breakfast, dew sparkling on the lawn, they were on the front porch in rockers. Ponder was perched on the rail, licking himself.

This moment was another chance to talk to Grandpa Pentreath, just the two of them, away from all ears. Maybe he'd have some answers. His father certainly hadn't been of help.

Evan said, "I don't have much courage."

"Part of courage is self-confidence."

"Were you as small as I am when you were eleven?"

"About the same size, I think," Tom said. "But smaller people have to be buzz saws."

Buzz saws? Like wasps.

"Did bigger kids in the neighborhood or at school beat you up?"

"Now and then, but I finally got tough."

"What did you do?"

"I hit 'em in the Adam's apple or punched 'em in the gut or kicked 'em you-know-where."

Evan's laugh was hollow. "Is that what I should do?"

"You can try."

"There's a guy named Mike Hodge who picks on me. Elbows me in the hallways and makes jokes about my foot, takes what he wants out of my lunch bag."

"I know the kind, Evander."

"He's a lot stronger and bigger than I am, and a head taller. He has red hair and pimples. I'm afraid of him. He delivers our paper and throws it at me when he can."

"Being small myself, I've had that problem a number of times in my life. The big guys have fun being bullies."

"What did you do, Grandpa?"

"Bided my time and when least expected, let 'em

have it. It had to get pretty bad before I did it. On ships, there's no place to go or hide. Enemies can throw you overboard. So I had to make sure the bully wouldn't bother me anymore. I'd hurt him enough to make sure."

"How did you hurt them?"

Tom searched his memory.

"Different ways, depending on the circumstances."

"What different ways?"

This boy was certainly persistent.

"There was a Yorkshireman on the *Porthleven* who hounded me unmercifully. He knocked me down several times with his right fist. One evening when the 'Yorkie' was having his meal and had his right hand down on the wooden table, I took my carpenter's mallet out and smashed his right knuckles. He couldn't make a fist."

"He didn't bother you after that?"

"No, he didn't."

"Tell me about other times."

Tom cleared his throat. "Evander, these aren't nice things to talk about, fighting and the like."

"Yes, they are, Grandpa. I can tell Buddy Jensen. I think he wishes you were his grandfather instead of the one he has near Richmond."

"Well, there was this brute on the *Northumberland,* the Portuguese cook who had a terrible temper. Every ship's cook is short of temper. Everyone complained about what he fixed, me most of all. One morning I said his food wasn't fit for the rats we had aboard. He grabbed a butcher knife and began chasing me over the deck. He was slow and clumsy, and I hid behind a hatch coaming and tripped him. When he fell he accidentally cut three of his own toes off."

Evan laughed.

"It wasn't a laughing matter, Evander. He had trouble balancing himself the rest of the voyage."

"Why was that?"

"Your toes give you balance. That Portuguese was sorry he'd whacked his own toes. When the ship rolled, he'd fall down."

"Grandpa, what do I do about Mike Hodge?"

Tom was silent for a while, thinking, then said, "Get a pair of your old pants and stuff the legs with straw, really pack them tight. Then get some red paint and draw a circle around you-know-where, then hang them up in the barn and think about Mike Hodge wearing them."

"After that?"

"Which leg is strongest?"

"My right one, the clubfoot leg. It has more muscles."

"Go out and practice every day kicking Mike Hodge between the legs, and if he bothers you on the first day of school, you know what to do. Don't miss."

"Yes, I'll know what to do. I won't miss."

T H E Y were now out at the tool bench in the barn,
Tom fixing the broken leg of a breakfast chair. He'd
already repaired a shelf in Jane's sewing room and re-
hung the barn doors, always open in the summer.

"Can I ask you another important question,
Grandpa?"

Tom nodded, applying glue before using a clamp.

"Those green and yellow snakes you have on your
forearms?"

"My tattoos?"

Evan nodded. "What kind of snakes are they?
They're ugly."

"Pit vipers. I'm no longer proud of them. I was at
the time I got them. Now I can't get rid of them.

They'll go with me when I'm buried at sea, in the old deep six."

"Where did you get them?"

"Island of Penang, in the Malacca Straits, below the Bay of Bengal and the Andaman Sea, across from Sumatra, off the Malay Peninsula."

Evan had never heard of those places. "'How did it happen?"

"With some shipmates I was staggering down Penang Road, where it turns into Campbell Street. We'd all had too much to drink. And there was this Chinese tat parlor. We all went in and got our skin art. That was the way of the young sailor in the eighteen hundreds. The landlubbers expected us to do that."

"Are pit vipers poisonous?"

"Very much so. There are thousands of them in the Malaysian jungles, along with tigers and leopards and monkeys. In fact, there are thousands of them in the Buddhist Temple of the Azure Cloud on the road south of George Town at Milestone 4. When you climb the hundred steps of the temple, you'll see the pit vipers all around you."

"Alive?"

Tom nodded. "On the altars, shrines, incense burners, candlesticks, vases, tables, underfoot and overhead. In fact, there's even a maternity tree where newborn vipers live, no bigger than worms. They slither all around it."

Evan made a face and said, "Gee."

"It's because of their kinship to the mythical dragons of Chinese folklore. Some people worship pit vipers. I certainly don't."

"I hope I don't dream about them tonight."

"I hope you don't, either."

"Wait'll I tell Buddy Jensen."

"We'll take him fishing tomorrow."

"Grandpa, a while ago you said you wanted to be buried at sea. Why is that?"

"I don't want to rot in the ground, turn into a skeleton down there. There's an old captain in New York named Scowcroft, one of my former skippers. He has a fund for sailors like me and takes care of our sea burials. Most sailors want to be buried on land, but not me."

"How do they do it?"

"They wrap you in a canvas bag, put some rocks

down at the feet, put you on a boat, go outside the harbor, say a mariner's prayer, and roll you overboard. Simple and quick. No funeral home, no embalming. The sea is much cleaner than the land."

"You're going to live a long time, Grandpa."

Tom smiled. "As rascally as I once was, I expect so."

Jane Bryant stuck her head out the back door. "Father, could I talk to you a moment? It's private, Evan."

Evan hobbled down the block to Buddy Jensen's house.

Buddy was in the backyard pulling weeds and dandelions. He earned his ten cents a week allowance that way.

Evan said, "You wouldn't believe this morning. He told me how to take care of Mike Hodge, told me about smashing a sailor's right hand with a wooden mallet, about how he cut a cook's toes off, and how he got those pit viper tattoos on his forearms. We're going fishing tomorrow, and you can ask him about all those things."

"What time are we going fishing?"

"I'll let you know."

"How did he say to take care of Mike Hodge?"

"Kick him in the crotch."

"Evan, that's dangerous." Buddy sat back in the grass.

"I know. I've got to practice all summer."

At the supper table, Evan said, "Grandpa told me how to take care of Mike Hodge. He said to kick him in the crotch the first day of school. I've got to practice all summer on a pair of pants stuffed with straw."

Howard Bryant almost choked on a mouthful of chicken salad. "Your grandfather told you to do *what?*"

Tom felt as though a ship were about to sink beneath him.

E VAN felt awful as his father said angrily, "Pentreath, you are to stop advising our son on how to conduct himself at school. Telling him to kick another student is an outrage."

"He came to me with a problem, Mr. Bryant."

"That was a mistake, and your solution was a worse mistake. I know all about Mike Hodge, and Evan would likely be beaten into a pulp because of your advice."

Evan's mother said, "Howard, my father meant well."

"Yes, he did," echoed Evan. The battleground was, again, supper. Why did they have to eat?

"Quiet, Evan," his father barked. "And while we're on the subject of interference, I'd appreciate your not telling any more of your sea stories to him. Jane says Evan now wants to become a sailor when he grows up. He's not physically fit. He's a cripple. And I can't imagine a more worthless profession."

Evan flinched. If any word hurt, it was "cripple."

"Somebody has to sail ships, Mr. Bryant," Tom said quietly.

Evan said, "I've asked him to tell me about all the places he's been and what he's done."

Gazing at Tom, Bryant snorted. "If your grandfather was a banker or a lawyer or a doctor or a college professor, I would quite agree."

Jane said, "Howard, can't you remember what it was like to be an eleven-year-old boy, growing up curious about everything? It's perfectly natural for Evan to ask about the sea and foreign lands."

"You're taking geography at school, aren't you, Evan?"

"Yes," Evan replied, barely audible.

"That should be enough to tell you about foreign lands."

Feeling he needed to defend Evander, Tom said, "It isn't the same as visiting them, Mr. Bryant."

"Speaking of foreign lands, are you a British citizen?"

"I am, sir."

Evan's father said, "Hmh. Are you in this country legally, may I ask?"

"No, Mr. Bryant, I am not legal here. I crossed the Canadian border without approval. I will not lie to you or my daughter or Evander."

"You know, Pentreath, I'm beginning to believe that there are other things we don't know about you, things beyond a sailor's usual drunkenness."

Evan said, "Please, Father . . ."

Tom stared at Bryant for a moment and then said, "I am an old man, and to tell you the complete story of my life would take days, and I realize my visit won't last that long. We'll go fishing tomorrow, and then I'll build the rowboat for Evander, then leave."

Evan couldn't hold it any longer. He shouted, "Father, why are you so mean?" He sprang up and hobbled out the back door. His chest was heaving.

"What's this about a rowboat? Who's going to pay for it?"

Jane said swiftly, "I am. I've saved almost sixty

dollars over the last four years. It will be Evan's birth-day gift."

"He's not strong enough to row a boat!"

"Yes, he is!" Tom said flatly, then added, "Excuse me, sir, excuse me, Jane," and followed his grandson outside. He found him weeping, his head nestled against Toby's warm neck.

Tom wrapped an arm around Evander's shoulder. "All that talk doesn't bother me; why should it bother you?"

"Why does he do it?"

"Because of me leaving your mother when she was a small child. You know all about that."

"She's forgiven you, Grandpa."

"But he hasn't."

The sun had set, and inside the barn, shadows were deepening. Tom said, "Let's sit down." A hay bale was a few feet away. "You'll soon feel better."

Evan sniffed, swallowed, and nodded. "On the streetcar that first day when we went to feed the pigeons, you said you'd been to Robinson Crusoe's island after taking a ship out of this harbor."

"I'm not supposed to tell you any more sea stories."

"Do it anyway," Evan said defiantly. "Please."

Tom hoped he wouldn't get into more trouble. "I was aboard the square-rigger *Martha Glover*, out of Boston, headed for San Francisco. At the foot of South America, Cape Horn gave us a pounding as usual, and then we stopped at San Fernandez Island, 360 miles off Chile, for fresh water. It hadn't rained since we left the Horn, and our barrels were practically empty."

"I thought it rained at sea all the time."

"There are places out there where it might not rain for weeks, and it might be that we wouldn't have any fresh water for hundreds of miles ahead until we got off tropic Ecuador. So we launched several longboats loaded with barrels. We rowed to shore. You know the Crusoe story?"

Evan nodded. "It's a novel."

"Supposedly based on truth. Alexander Selkirk, a Scotchman, was put ashore after arguing with the captain of the galley *Cinque Ports* around 1700. He lived alone on the main island for four years and four months until he was rescued by a British man-o'-war."

"Then Daniel Defoe wrote his story, didn't he?"

Evan said. "I love it, Robinson Crusoe with his Man Friday and his parrot."

"I went to the cave where Selkirk lived and to his lookout rock. When he landed he said he saw dozens of shipwrecked cats. We saw hundreds. The island is covered with trees and giant green ferns where hummingbirds nest. We picked wild fruits, took big lobsters from the rocks, and loaded our barrels with water from falls thundering down from the mountains."

"What did you do then?" Evan couldn't get enough of the sea stories. He wanted to hear them again and again.

"Rowed back to the ship and soon set sail before sundown. The waters are dangerous, and the currents are fast. Dozens of ships have wrecked on the rocks. Whalers, pirates, and ships like the *Martha Glover*."

"I have to go there someday, Grandpa."

"Most things are possible, Evan. Think about that," Tom said. "Most things are possible."

Tom and Evan talked on for a while, then returned inside the house, Tom climbing upstairs and Evan heading for his room. His parents were still at the dining table. It was obvious they'd been arguing, something they seldom did. His mother usually walked away from disagreements.

Evan paused in the hallway as she said, "I never thought for a moment that you'd behave this way. You're acting childish; you're not only hurting me, but you're hurting Evan, too. It's no business of yours or mine whether or not he's legal. . . ." She was saying it with a coldness Evan had never heard.

Evan waited for his father to reply. There was only silence.

"And another thing, Howard. I never again want to hear you call our son a 'cripple.' You've done it several times in the past. Do it once more and I'll leave you and take Evan with me. . . ."

Evan felt a surge of admiration for his mother. She was finally fighting back.

"Jane, it's just a word —"

"An ugly word. Never again, Howard. . . ."

Evan walked to his room, slipped inside, and closed the door, feeling good about his mother.

Tom got into bed and read for a while from a book

about the American Civil War that he'd borrowed from
the Bryants' library shelf, his glasses perched on his nose.

He heard steps on the stairs and then a knock. He
said, "Come in," expecting Evander.

His daughter opened the door and sat down on the side of the bed. "I'm so ashamed over Howard's performance tonight. He said he'd apologize, but I don't think he will."

"He doesn't really need to," Tom said. "I shouldn't have told Evander to kick Mike Hodge."

"Yes, he does need to apologize. You're my father, and you're a guest in *our* house, and you don't deserve this treatment."

"I'll be going soon, and your lives will return to normal. I'm just so happy that you allowed me to come."

"You have no idea what your visit has meant to me and Evan."

"That feeling is mutual. He's a wonderful, loving boy, and meeting the both of you is the highlight of my life."

Jane leaned over and kissed his forehead, bidding him good night and a good sleep.

After she left, Tom wondered whether or not he should have told her about the Hartlepool *and* Dartmoor *this night, this time. He felt guilty.*

Unable to sleep after the conversation at the supper table, Evander's clash with his father, and Jane's visit, Tom got out of bed after midnight and dressed to take a walk up Hoople toward High Street. He tiptoed down the steps and eased the front door open.

Though warm, it was a lovely night. The heavens were crammed with stars. As he walked slowly, he picked out Alpheratz, Deneb Kaitos, Achernar, Aldebaran, *and* Sirius, *old friends of the dark blue-ink sky. The dragon-headed cane tapped along.*

The lights were out in Mr. Faircloth's mansion.

The visit wasn't turning out the way he'd hoped. Yet it was. Just being around his daughter and grandson for a short while was enough, despite the husband.

He limped along for almost two hours, eased himself back into the house, and quickly fell asleep.

12

E V A N awakened before dawn after a mostly troubled sleepless night, anticipating the day. At long last, he'd go fishing again. With that dumb foot, he didn't have many chances to do special things. This was one he could do. He couldn't wait.

He dressed quickly and went to the barn to feed Toby, Woody, and the chickens. He said to Woody, "Guess where I'm going," filling Toby's feed box with oats, scattering grain for the already clucking hens, out of their coops.

Returning to the kitchen, he found his mother in her summer robe, starting coffee. It was early for her to be up.

He said, "I can't wait to go. Should I wake Grandpa?"

"I think I heard him upstairs. Your lunches are in the icebox."

"You fixed one for Buddy?"

"Of course I did. I'll get your breakfast."

Soon, thick strips of bacon were frying in the iron skillet.

Evan sat down at the table.

"With Grandpa being a professional, I have a feeling we're going to catch a lot today."

She smiled at him. "I do, too."

"I'll bet he knows where they're biting."

"I'll bet so, too."

Then she walked over to stand by him, looking down at him. "I'm sorry about last night. I made your father promise he'd apologize to my father and to you."

"He should. I don't understand what he has against Grandpa."

"Again, it's the fact that he didn't get in touch with me for years, and your father doesn't like sailors. He considers them crude and violent. It takes a long time for your father to change about anything."

Just then, Tom came down the steps, saying cheerfully, "That bacon is making the chow bell ring, just like it did on ships."

He limped across the kitchen and bestowed a kiss on his daughter's cheek and said, "Top o' the mornin', Evander. Are you ready for a voyage?"

"I can't wait, Grandpa."

They were soon on their way.

Tom paid the fifteen cents, a nickel each, for the trolley ride down High Street to the ferry landing, listening to the excited chatter of Evander and Buddy Jensen. What a privilege it would have been to have two young sons of his own and take them fishing, hear them talking about it.

They got off the trolley at the Crawford Street intersection, by the railroad tracks, and walked over to the fish docks to buy a dime's worth of dead shrimp for bait. Then they caught the bulky side-paddle ferry, a nickle each, to Norfolk across the sluggish Elizabeth River.

Evan said, "I used a bamboo pole and bobbin the times before."

"Hand-lining is simpler," Tom said.

No lugging bamboo poles on the streetcar they'd have to take on the long ride to Ocean View Beach on the Chesapeake Bay.

The morning before he'd bought line for a quarter and had wrapped fifty-foot lengths around three pieces of wood five inches long. He'd paid a dime for ten Number 4 hooks and another dime for five lead sinkers, watching his money carefully. Pennies counted more than ever.

"You put the weight on the bottom of the line, attach the hook about a foot up to a ten-inch leader that I'll make, wait until the sinker hits the bottom, then pull it up about six inches. Use your forefinger to feel the tug; hook the fish by jerking up. It's that simple."

Another trolley to Ocean View for a dime each, and then he rented a rowboat all day for a dollar. Total investment so far, $2.15. Another sixty cents to get home.

Evander and Buddy had a burlap bag each to take their catch back to Hoople Street.

At the boat rental shack he asked where the fish were biting that day. "Out at the wreck buoy." He could see a half dozen boats gathered about a half mile offshore. Fish usually hung around wrecks. He began rowing that way. The boys sat on the stern sheet, anxious to drop their lines.

About midway, he felt sharp chest pains, grimaced, and stopped rowing, reaching into his shirt pocket for the nitro pill box, chewing one.

"Are you all right, Grandpa?" Evan asked.

"Just indigestion," Tom answered, taking in a deep breath, waiting for the stabs to end.

"Are you sure?"

"I'm fine," Tom said. *This wasn't the right time or place for a heart attack. He remembered Captain Scowcroft's dire prediction. He'd die in Portsmouth.*

"Will our boat be like this one?" asked Evan.

Our boat! That brought a smile to Tom's face.

"A lot like this one. We'll use cedar for the planking and oak for the keel and knees, the ribs. Pine for the seats. Pine is cheaper."

"What color shall we paint it?"

We! "Up to you, matey."

Tom hadn't been at oars since rescue days when the Trethellan *had gone down in Mount's Bay, and his hands, mostly unused since he'd taken up residence at the International Seaman's Last Harbor, were soft and would blister, he knew. That was a minor problem.*

But it was good to get out on the water again. Maybe he should take another voyage, but many of the steamers didn't carry carpenters anymore; didn't really need them. He didn't think he'd ever see the day when sailing ships would no longer dominate the seas. Most were now tied up and rotting while the smoky hulls carried the cargoes and passengers. Sailors like himself were made to feel useless.

His thoughts were jarred when Evander said, "Grandpa, when can we stop and fish?"

"Just a few minutes more." They were approaching the wreck buoy. "Bait up."

Tom really couldn't remember the first time he'd gone fishing out of Mousehole on his father's boat, but he thought he couldn't have been more than three. He'd gone out every trip that he didn't have to go to school, until his father drowned off Brisson's Rocks in January 1851, when he was seven.

He tossed the anchor overboard and said, "Let 'em go," and the boys, eyes alight, sent their weights to the bottom, Evan shifting to the bow seat. Tom had tied off their burlap bags to cleats on the rails to get them wet, ready to receive the fish.

In less than a minute, Buddy Jensen yelled, "I've got one," and Tom said, "Haul it up, hand over hand." The wriggling Ocean View spot, silver-gray with yellowish bars, was about twelve inches long, a member of the snapper family.

Then Evan shouted. He'd hooked up.

It went that way for the next five hours. The spot, and bigger croakers, were plentiful near the buoy, but Tom warned, "Sometimes you could come to a place like this and not catch even one."

Buddy Jensen said, "That happened the time before last in Hampton Roads."

Evan said, "Grandpa, tell Buddy the stories you've told me about the sea rescues, the pigeons in New Guinney as big as turkeys, the blue ones in the Comoro Islands, and how you got your tattoos of pit vipers on the Malaysian island. . . ."

Buddy said, "Is that true about pigeons as big as turkey birds?"

"Oh, yes."

Evan listened to the retold stories.

With thirty-some fish aboard, including three croakers and two striped bass, they started back for shore about four o'clock. Tom rowed slowly. *He was relieved when the prow crunched up on the soft sand, his promise to Evander fulfilled, a day he'd remember until he died.*

When they returned home, Evan went to his room, and on the bed were a pair of old trousers, packed hard with straw, a red circle around the crotch. His mother had tied string at the cuff of each leg, and she had sewn the waist shut after placing two grommets for the suspension line.

Evan went out to thank her. *Look out, Mike Hodge.*

13

ABOUT ten in the morning, when Jane was making the beds, she heard a voice calling out through the front door screen, "Anyone at home?" She answered and began walking up the hall.

Two middle-aged men were standing on the porch, one in a police uniform, the other plainclothes. He was wearing a Panama straw hat. The one in plainclothes said, "Mrs. Bryant, I don't want to shock you or scare you, but Mr. Faircloth was murdered last night, and we'd like to ask a few questions." He introduced himself as Detective Gordon, Portsmouth Police.

That was impossible! Her breath had caught.

"Murdered?" Mr. Faircloth lived eight doors away.

"Yes, ma'am. His body was discovered by the cook when she came to the house about seven. He'd been beaten and stabbed, and there's evidence that he was robbed."

"Oh, my Lord, here in this neighborhood? I can't believe it."

"Neither can anyone else. Have you seen any suspicious people around here lately?" He was potbellied. He had a mustache and was sweating profusely. His shirt was wet.

"No. This is a very quiet, close neighborhood. We all know each other. We seldom see strangers of any kind."

"Mrs. Bryant, two of your neighbors say that your father is here visiting you from New York." Anyone from New York was considered a foreigner in Portsmouth.

Jane frowned. "Yes, he arrived four days ago." She'd told the neighbors.

"Is he here now? We have to check everyone."

"He went to the lumberyard with our son, Evan.

They're starting to build a boat this afternoon. They left about an hour ago and should be back soon."

"May I have his name, please?" He opened his notebook.

"Pentreath, Thomas Pentreath." She spelled it out. "My father is seventy years old. Surely you don't suspect him."

"No, no. Not at all. We're just checking everyone in the area; man, woman, and child. I'll come back later to talk to your father."

The Model T Ford touring car pulled away from the front of 960 Hoople Street, and Jane went inside, weak-kneed, heart beating rapidly, to sit down in the living room. Mr. Faircloth was one of the most influential men in town. Trying to calm down, Jane sat for at least ten minutes. Who could have done this terrible thing? Jane knew Mr. Faircloth by sight. He was always cordial, tipping his hat, smiling. He was a large man with a florid face.

Out in the kitchen to mix a glass of ice water, she heard the buggy jangle up the driveway and went through the back door. Seldom was anyone murdered in Portsmouth. There was little crime in the small city.

Evan had already parked in front of the barn to unload the wood, and her father had slid down, saying to her, "I think we have everything we need."

Evan said, "Mama, what's going on at the Faircloth house? A whole bunch of people are standing around outside."

"Mr. Faircloth was murdered last night. The police were already here."

Evan's mouth had fallen open. His eyes were big. "You mean he's dead?"

"Yes, Evan. Detective Gordon said he was beaten and stabbed. He said robbery might be involved."

"In this nice neighborhood?" Tom commented, frowning.

Jane said, "I feel ill."

Buddy Jensen walked up. "You know what's going on, Evan?"

"I just heard."

"We live even closer to him than you do," Buddy said.

Evan said, "Help me with this lumber. We're going to start after lunch."

"I went up there. Everyone was talking about all the blood in his bedroom," Buddy Jensen said.

"That's what happens when you get stabbed," Evan said.

His mother said, "Stay away from Mr. Faircloth's house, both of you."

They began unloading the boards. Then Evan moved the buggy behind the barnyard fence, letting Toby escape the traces.

Tom said, "I'll make a couple of sawhorses. We'll build it on them."

Buddy Jensen said, "I said hello to him day before yesterday as he was backing his car out of the driveway." Mr. Faircloth's Stutz was the only car on the street.

Tom said, "I was thinking last night that we should make the boat ten feet long instead of twelve. It'll be easier for you to handle and a little lighter. You'll either have to buy or build a cart for Toby to haul it to the river."

The western branch of the Elizabeth was six blocks away. "We'll make a cart," Evan said.

Buddy Jensen said, pulling a cedar board from the back of the buggy, "I wonder if it was somebody who knew Mr. Faircloth took a lot of money home with him at night?"

Evan said, "Buddy, I haven't any idea." His mind was on the boat.

"Maybe somebody has been watching him after he left the bank every day?"

Evan said, "Buddy, I'm sorry about Mr. Faircloth, but we have a job to do here."

Amused at the conversation, Tom said, "Yes, we do," and began using Mr. Bryant's handsaw, which he'd sharpened, to cut a pine two-by-four and begin a sawhorse.

14

A little after one, the black Model T touring car again parked in front of the Bryants' house, and Detective Gordon came up the walk. Jane directed him to the backyard, following him there.

He introduced himself and shook hands with Tom. They stepped into the shade, Gordon taking out his notebook, beginning to ask questions: Where did Tom live in New York? How long had he been at his daughter's house? Tom seemed a little bewildered, Evan thought.

Evan and his mother, and Buddy Jensen, stood a few feet away, listening. Evan had never even been near a detective, much less hearing one. He didn't like the way the detective stared at his grandfather, the tone of his voice.

Then Detective Gordon said, "I seem to detect an accent."

"I'm British."

"May I see your visa?"

Tom reddened. "I don't have one, sir."

Gordon said, "How did you get into this country?"

"I crossed the Canadian border three years ago." *He hadn't expected anything like this to happen.*

"That's up to the immigration people to handle, but I will have to report you."

What a stupid thing for me to do, he thought. There were thousands of foreign sailors living in the U.S.A., and this old salt had just been caught. He glanced over at Evander and his mother, at Buddy Jensen. They had worried looks, they knew he was in trouble. They were right.

"Have you ever been arrested in this country?"

"No, sir." That was truthful.

Tom already knew what the next question would be and was sweating even more than Detective Gordon. He might even be looking guilty of killing the neighbor.

"Have you ever been arrested in any country?"

Tom felt like the earth was opening beneath his feet and that he'd plunge down an endless chasm. "I was once arrested at sea on a voyage from Australia to England. Many, many years ago."

"For what crime?"

Tom wished his daughter and grandson were a million miles away, instead of ten feet.

He took a long breath, and answered, "I killed a man in self-defense." He was looking at his daughter and Evander as he said it. *Captain Scowcroft had been right. Tell them the first day.*

Jane's hand went up to her mouth, and Evander reacted as though he'd been hit with a hammer. He began shaking his head in disbelief. His own grandpa a murderer.

"Were you convicted?"

"Yes, sir, I was. In a maritime court in Bristol, England."

"Did you do time?"

"Yes, sir, I did. I was sentenced to twenty years but was released in eleven for good behavior."

"Where did you serve the time?"

"Dartmoor."

"Ouch! Dartmoor is known as one of the worst prisons on earth. Only the worst convicts are there."

Totally subdued, Tom said, "It was not a good experience." *He felt ill. Why hadn't he told Jane in the very first letter he'd sent to her? Why, oh why?*

"How did you kill the victim?"

"I beat him to death with a belaying pin. He threatened to throw me overboard during a storm."

Gordon shook his head. "We do have a problem here, and I'm not sure it will get better. I don't have a budget for a telegraph to Scotland Yard requesting information, but because Mr. Faircloth was so well known, I'll have the chief find the money."

Tom remained silent. Scotland Yard, home of British crime fighters, was in London. The court records were in Bristol. Telegraph was the new miracle. He'd also heard about something called radio.

"Because you're so old, I won't arrest you on suspicion of murder, but I'm confining you to this property until we finish the investigation."

"Thank you," Tom said. "I didn't do it, Mr. Gordon."

"By the way, where were you last night?"

"I was here."

Gordon said slowly, "We do have a problem, Mr. Pentreath. Do you own a knife?"

"Yessir, I do."

"When was the last time you used it?"

"Late yesterday, to clean fish. I'd taken my grandson and his friend to Ocean View."

"Where is the knife?"

"Up in my seabag."

"Would you please get it for me?"

Tom nodded and went into the house.

"I'm sorry about this," Detective Gordon said to Evan's mother. Disbelief was in her eyes. Shock.

His face white and agonized, Evan said, "My grandpa didn't do it. He didn't."

Mouth wide open, Buddy Jensen was speechless.

"Let's hope not," said the detective.

Tom returned with the knife. *Many sailors carried them as a tool of the profession. The blade was about four inches long.*

Gordon examined it and said, "Where did you say you used it last?"

Tom thought a moment. He hadn't said where he used it.

"Down by the creek."

Gordon opened it to look at the blade and stepped into the sunlight for a closer look. "There seems to be fresh blood on the handle."

"I guess I didn't wash it off very well," Tom said. "I was tired after a day on the water."

Gordon's eyes held Tom as if he were trying to see inside his head. Finally, he said, "I'll take this with me, Mr. Pentreath. Thank you for your time." He tipped his Panama hat to Jane and walked by the side of the house out to the street.

Tom sank down on the grass and put his head between his knees. Finally, he lifted it and told his daughter, his grandson, and Buddy Jensen about the terrible night on the *Hartlepool*.

The four-masted bark had sailed from Sydney, thirty-eight hundred tons of wheat aboard, bound for delivery in Bristol. It was Tom's second voyage on her. He'd suffered from the constant harassment of big Ozzie O'Brien during the first voyage. The Belfast bo'sun had taken instant dislike, for reasons unknown, the moment he saw smallish Tom Pentreath. Maybe he didn't like the pug face or the Cornish accent? Maybe he didn't like the fearless look in Tom's eyes? Maybe he knew the little Cornishman would brook no petty nonsense? The hatred was open.

It all began peacefully with a "Godspeed" from the steam tug that towed her out of port in light winds, her great sails up and ballooning as the winds increased. She sailed along in silence except for the creaking of her top hamper, fretting of her gear aloft and the hissing of her hull.

Four days later, when heavy storm clouds blanked out the Southern Cross, and gale winds roared, her master yelled, "All hands on deck, stand-by topgallant halyards." Seas were crashing over the main deck. A little after the topgallants were clewed and bunted, the order was shouted, "Lay aloft and furl . . ."

The seas were thundering, the Hartlepool rising and falling on the water mountains, the winds screeching at probably eighty miles an hour. Tom was clinging to a lifeline rigged across the deck, water washing up to his knees. He'd suffered a fractured right ankle the day before and couldn't climb. Big Ozzie, in his oilskins, ugly face slick with rain, knew that; he knew that Tom might well fall sixty feet with one misstep, and he shouted, "Lay aloft, Chips, or I'll throw you overboard. . . ."

"Send me to my death, you Irish pig?" Tom shouted back.

His big hands extended, Ozzie came for Evan's grandpa to toss him into the raging sea.

Tom reached behind him for a belaying pin, a wood-handled steel pin used in making lines fast. Ozzie's hands were only a foot from Tom's shoulders when the belaying pin hit him in the forehead, caving his skull. He collapsed like a bag of the cargo, his head a bloody mess. He was dead, washing back and forth in the foaming scuppers.

That was what the captain saw. Saw nothing else, only the killing. In the howl of the wind, he hadn't heard the words, the threat; he didn't know that Tom's right ankle was broken. All he saw was his favorite boatswain being beaten to death.

He ordered the chief mate to arrest Tom Pentreath, of Mousehole, and take him to the tiny lazaret belowdecks, which functioned as a jail. Tom stayed down there on "bread and water," hardtack and a pint of water a day, for ninety days until the bark docked in Bristol. During that time, he managed to splint his broken ankle and bind it with wood and cloth smuggled in by friends. By the time the Hartlepool made England, the bones had healed crookedly, never to be the same again. But he walked down the gangway, in handcuffs, as if the foot was perfect, pain screaming in his temples. He would die before he would let the cruel master see him limp. The word amongst the crew was that Tom was a very tough little man.

The court took the master's eyewitness account of a brutal murder at the height of a storm where the ship required the skill of every crewman aboard her.

When Tom said his ankle was broken and he could not go aloft, the master testified, "Why, he walked off my vessel with all the cockiness he had when he came aboard."

Off to Dartmoor Prison without further words.

15

B U D D Y Jensen went away shaking his head.

Evan dreaded the thought of his father coming home from the shoe store; so did his mother, he knew. Evan said, "Do we have to tell him?"

Tom said instantly, "Yes, we do."

Jane added, "Absolutely."

Tom said, "Evander, I'll ask his forgiveness. I did not mean to bring all this down on the only family I have." *What would the neighbors think?*

They'd returned inside the house and were in the living room, still stunned, dazed by what had happened, not knowing exactly where to be, what to say. Evan's father would arrive not long after six.

Tom had seen the living room but had not been in it.

There were two sofas, two padded chairs, a Victrola upon which to play records, and a piano. There was a handsome Oriental rug on the hardwood flooring. There were two oil paintings on the walls. There were some purple silk flowers in one vase, roses in another.

He'd never been in a room like it and again knew he had no business being here, a lowly sailor, Dartmoor convict. Perhaps the best thing to do was to write a note thanking the Bryants for their love and hospitality, then slip away in the darkness and return to Brooklyn. If the immigration people found him there at ISLH and deported him back to England, it would be what he deserved. Maybe the New York police would arrest him on suspicion of murder and send him back to Portsmouth. Yes, the best thing to do was slip away.

The doorbell rang, and Jane got up to answer it at the screen door. Tom and Evan heard her say, "I'm sorry. He's not available just now. But I can tell you, without any doubt, my father did not kill Mr. Faircloth."

"Who was that?" Evan asked.

"A reporter and a photographer from the newspaper."

"We'll be in the paper tomorrow?" he asked.

She said, "The police must have told them something."

Tom shook his head. What next? Now would be a good time to have a fatal heart attack.

Evan's mother said, "I have to fix supper," and went to the kitchen.

Evan said, "Grandpa, are there any other bad things that we should know about?"

Tom sighed. "None that would involve your family."

Tom had known about Dartmoor since his youth. Of all prisons on earth, in any English-speaking country, it had the worst reputation, home to the worst murderers of the British Isles.

At one time, the "hellship prisons," old dismasted men-of-war anchored off Portsmouth and Plymouth, contained the violent population, confined belowdecks, often in chains, breathing stale air, coughing all night when the hatches were closed. Death was by the daily dozen. Dartmoor had inherited the surviving convicts, had inherited him.

Cruelty of the warders, the guards, ruled the prison and extended to the child convicts, some as young as twelve, often tormented, often molested.

Tom was marched out of Bristol Court in chains, the way he'd gone in, and was transported by train to the bleak, cold mystical moors of Devon, in southern England, finally by horse-drawn wagon to feared Dartmoor. He was wearing the same clothes he'd worn the wild night he'd killed Ozzie O'Brien on the Hartlepool, *140 days before.*

The sky was overcast, usual for the misty summers of silent Dartmoor, with its circular double walls of moorstone, mixed with granite. Inside the circle were six three-story cell blocks, with doors of sheet iron.

Tom was issued his uniform of a short, loose jacket and vest, with black striped baggy knickers of drab tweed. His legs were encased in worsted stockings with bright red convict rings around them. The clothing was stamped with red "prisoner" arrows. Even his boots had nails in the shape of an arrow, easy to track on the moors.

What hit him like a chill sponge was the total profound silence once he passed through the main entrance gate. He'd been warned. Silence meant no talking, night or day, no whispering, no nodding of heads. Punishment was quick and severe. Solitary confinement on bread and water for three days.

For major offenses there was the cat-o'-nine-tails, a whip with nine leather lashes across the shoulders and back; the birch rod, much more painful on naked buttocks. Tom soon felt both.

He was marched to the "punishment block" five times and spent nine months in solitary confinement in a bare cell picking at tarred rope with only the Bible and a prayer book to read. This all occurred within his first two years at Dartmoor when anger boiled over at being confined for killing in self-defense. He attempted to escape.

The food was better than at the time of the 1809 French war and the War of 1812 with America. Unlucky, unruly Americans were imprisoned at Dartmoor.

For breakfast, gruel and bread; for dinner, boiled meat or soup, potatoes and bread; for supper, cocoa

and bread. Tom, always hungry, sometimes ate his cell
candles.

Labor for the half-starved convicts was breaking
stones for road making and prison repair or digging
peat, sometimes standing in water two feet deep. Cloth
bags instead of gloves were issued to cover hands in
winter. Water trickled down in many of the unheated
cells, and snow covered the window ledges. The freez-
ing silver fog of Dartmoor was legendary. Thousands
had died since the first prisoners had arrived in spring
of 1809.

Tom survived out of sheer defiance and fed the visit-
ing pigeons with bread scraps he smuggled out of the
convict's mess.

Yet Dartmoor had changed him, as it would any
man, and perhaps he should tell about that terrible
part of his life on paper when he returned to Brooklyn
and mail it to his daughter for keeping until Evander
was older. That would be the honest way to do it.

He did not wish to talk about it this evening.

A familiar voice sounded from the front porch.
"Mrs. Bryant?"

Evan got up and went to the window. The police car was again parked in front of the house.

Jane answered, "Coming."

Evan went out into the hallway and saw Detective Gordon and two uniformed policemen at the door. He said, "Grandpa, the detective has come back."

Tom sat there, not replying. To Evan he seemed smaller than he was in the morning. His face was gray.

His mother said to the detective, "What now, Mr. Gordon?"

"I'm sorry to bother you again, but I'd like to speak to your father."

She said, tiredly, "Come in."

So close to childbirth, she did not need trouble of any kind. The baby was kicking again.

"This will only take a minute," he said and followed her to the living room, trailed by the policemen. Tom was still on the couch and looked up when they entered.

"Mr. Pentreath, this afternoon you told me that you were here last night."

"I was."

"A while ago, Mr. Jensen said he was on his front porch, rocking, having a pipe just after midnight, and saw a figure coming up the street, walking with a cane. Do you walk with a cane?"

Evan couldn't contain himself. "That's Buddy's daddy."

"Yes, I do," Tom admitted.

"Why did you lie to me? You did leave the house, didn't you?"

"I forgot. I honestly forgot." *He honestly had forgotten.*

"Mr. Pentreath, I have to arrest you for the murder of John Faircloth, and I have a warrant to search the room where you've been sleeping."

Jane said, "This is ridiculous," and Evan broke into tears.

Gordon continued, "In accordance with our department procedure involving felonies, I have to handcuff you."

Jane protested. "He's seventy years old!"

Tom arose silently and held out his wrists. *He hadn't been arrested since a bar brawl in Rangoon, several years after Dartmoor.*

Evan shouted, "No!" and moved to stand in front of his grandfather.

Gordon gently pushed him aside, saying, "Son, don't cause trouble."

His mother said, "Evan, don't interfere."

After the handcuffs clicked and Tom was placed in custody of the policemen, Gordon said, "Now, Mrs. Bryant, could you please show me where Mr. Pentreath has been staying?"

Evan's father walked up as Tom was being placed in the Model T, the newspaper photographer aiming his camera.

L O N G after the search was over and the police had gone, after supper, the shock remained. Evan's mother told his father what she remembered from the afternoon about the killing at sea. "He insisted it was self-defense. I have to believe him."

Evan's father was silent.

Evan's mother said, "We can't abandon him."

His father didn't answer.

Thinking about his grandpa in police headquarters and the jail, Evan decided to keep his mouth shut, hoping his father wouldn't suddenly rant and rage. Sometimes in the past, Evan had gotten into the middle of their conversations and suffered.

But his father seemed beaten down this night, withdrawn. Finally, he said, "Jane, you know I have a good business here, and I don't know how all this will affect it. We'll be in the paper tomorrow."

The words from each of them came slowly and thoughtfully, Evan noticed.

Finally, she said, "It seems to me that everyone will think well of you if you defend my father. You know he didn't do it. He didn't kill Mr. Faircloth."

Evan thought, yes, that's it. *He didn't do it, and shouldn't be in jail.* He said, "I'm going to bed." He thought they could talk much easier if he weren't there. They both said good night in sad voices.

As he left the dining room, he heard his father say, "I'm not sure how you want me to defend him."

Evan stopped and turned. "You could hire a lawyer." He had to say it. He had to.

Evan then went out back and sat down on the steps, Woody immediately running up to him, as usual. He scrubbed the dog's head and said, "We've got to figure a way to get him out." He'd heard about giving prisoners hacksaws to cut the bars.

In the early moonlight he could see the stacked

lumber and the sawhorses for building the boat. But the boat meant little to him now. He could only think of his grandpa. Nothing else. How he didn't deserve what was happening to him.

If he'd come three weeks earlier or three weeks later, he wouldn't have been blamed. If he hadn't taken that midnight walk, if Mr. Jensen hadn't seen him, he might not be in trouble. Just bad luck, all the way around. Detective Gordon needed a suspect, and old Thomas Pentreath from Mousehole was handy. Evan wondered how long they could keep him in jail? Try him?

He gave Woody a final raking with his fingers, said good night to him, and went back inside, knowing he'd fight sleep. Going over and over the day, he didn't drift off until early morning, sleeping in until after his father had gone to the store.

At breakfast, he said to his mother, "I'm going down to see him this morning."

She said, "I'll go this afternoon. I have a lawyer appointment at ten o'clock. Mr. Levy. I was so upset and confused after he was arrested that I didn't make up a package for him. His razor, toothbrush; personal things. I'll bring a change of clothes when I go, if he has one."

A little later, Evan took the cloth shopping bag with his grandfather's things inside it and went off up Hoople, stopping by Buddy Jensen's house to say, "You know your daddy didn't have to tell on Grandpa."

Buddy said, "He didn't even know who it was, just some man going by with a cane."

Evan kept on limping up Hoople. Humidity was high, and rain threatened. Evan felt as gray as the sky and talked to himself all the way to High Street, mostly about Detective Gordon. Why didn't he go about arresting criminals his own age? The trolley rocked and clanged on toward the business district.

The old brick jail and police headquarters were on Water Street, just above the Seaboard Railroad Terminal and the fish docks. Evan had seen it many times before but had never been inside.

He said to the police sergeant at the desk, "My grandpa is in a cell here, and I want to see him," not hiding his anger.

"What's his name?"

"Thomas Pentreath. He's been accused of killing Mr. Faircloth, but he didn't do it."

"We know he didn't do it! He's sitting outside Mr. Gordon's office, waiting for someone to take him home."

"He's not in a cell?"

"Boy, did you hear what I just said? He's down the hall. That way."

Evan couldn't believe what he was hearing, but not fifty feet away was his grandfather on a wooden bench. He got up when he saw Evan, his pug face screwed up in a Cheshire cat grin.

"Evander!"

"Grandpa!" Evan practically shouted.

They hugged right there in the jail hallway, outside Detective Gordon's door. The detective was inside, on the phone.

Tom said, "They caught the real killer. A bank clerk. He confessed about three hours ago. They woke me up to tell me."

"I knew you didn't do it. I said that to everyone, but I was real scared."

Tom said, "I asked the jailer for an outside cell so I could feed the pigeons."

Detective Gordon got off the phone and stepped out of his office, saying to Evan, "You two get out of here. This is no place for nice people."

Evan asked, "Why did the bank clerk do it?"

"Everyone knows what a skinflint Faircloth was," said the detective. "He paid that man five dollars for a six-day week and fired him when he asked for fifty cents more a day. They got into an argument. Sad story. Go home! I've been up all night and need to go home myself." With that he went back into his office, then came out again. "Mr. Pentreath, you've been through enough. I won't tell the immigration people about you. Behave yourself." As he disappeared again, Tom thanked him.

Evan said, "He didn't apologize."

Tom said, "I'm free. That's all that counts."

As they passed by the sergeant's desk Tom said cheerfully, "Top o' the day to you." He even swaggered a bit.

Outside, Evan said to his grandfather, "We're going to the newspaper office. It's on High Street."

"Why are we going there?"

"To make sure they have the right story. You were photographed yesterday with handcuffs on. We have to make sure people know you didn't do it. This is a gabby town."

Tom said, "If it makes you happy . . ."

A few minutes later, Tom was being interviewed, and a picture of them together was taken. "It'll be on the front page this afternoon. In fact, the whole front page will be about Mr. Faircloth's murder," they were told.

"Next stop, Evander Bryant Shoes,'" Evan said. The store was three blocks away, near Court. He wanted to make sure his father knew about the real killer, not wait for gossip or the newspaper.

Passing a bakery, Tom said, "Let's celebrate by feeding the pigeons." They went inside and bought a loaf of stale bread for a nickel.

At Evander Bryant Shoes, Evan saw his father breathe a sigh of relief that was enough to float a passenger balloon. He shook Tom's hand, slapped him on the back, and almost kissed him. Evan was amazed. Howard Bryant was a shrewd businessman,

Evan knew, and his father quickly saw that the whole affair had promotional advantages.

Several customers were in the store, and Howard loudly announced that the police had captured the real killer of John Faircloth, not his father-in-law.

Next to the final stop was the office of Abraham Levy, which was on the second floor above Evander Bryant Shoes. Both Mr. Levy and Evan's mother were openmouthed when Evan and his grandfather strode into the room. Mr. Levy had lost a client.

The final stop was the Confederate Statue and the pigeons.

As they sat at the base of the statue tearing off chunks of bread, Tom said, "You know, yesterday was like the time I was shanghaied. That's an old sailor's term for being kidnapped."

"You were once kidnapped?"

Tom nodded. "In 1889, the last days of the terrible Barbary Coast in San Francisco. You remember I told you I crewed on the *Martha Glover*? We went from the Robinson Crusoe island off Chile to Cocos Island, three hundred miles off Costa Rica, also to get fresh water, then proceeded north."

"I remember."

"Back in those days, there was trouble getting enough hands for the voyages to China. So there were gangs in San Francisco headed by masterminds who owned bars and boardinghouses and supplied sailors for sixty dollars per man. I was unfortunate enough to get into Miss Puckett's establishment. Flat chested, she had no teeth, and her lips and her chinbone were separated only by a half inch. She smoked cigarillos. She ran a 'shanghai' gang."

"A woman did that?"

Tom nodded. "She made me a drink of whiskey, gin, brandy, and sleeping potion. Then she knocked me over the head and slipped me through a trapdoor. I woke up on a ship leaving the Golden Gate, bound for Shanghai. I jumped overboard and swam to a Spanish ship inbound."

"How did you know she hit you over the head?"

"There was a big knot on it."

Another story for Buddy Jensen.

Eventually, they went home, a joyous occasion.

THE newspaper was delivered in late afternoon by Mike Hodge on his bicycle. Rubber banded, Mike aimed it at Evan's head. It was like a rock and bounced off his forehead, above his right eye, stinging and leaving a mark. Evan had been waiting on the front steps for more than an hour to read the Faircloth stories.

Mike shouted, "Your grandfather killed a man," and pumped away.

Some day, some sensational day, Evan didn't know when, but he'd surely get Mike Hodge. Yes, his grandfather had killed a man in self-defense.

The whole front page was filled with the Faircloth story except for a column telling about Thomas

"Chips" Pentreath. There was a picture of Pentreath and Evan Bryant, smiling widely after the sailor's release from jail. They were famous, and Evan ran inside to show it to his mother. His grandpa was still asleep upstairs after all the excitement.

Jane said, "All's well that ends well," smiling broadly.

Evan walked over to Buddy Jensen's house. Buddy was already reading the front page.

"Daddy's name isn't even mentioned here."

"Why should it be?"

"Well, he was questioned by that detective."

"Yeah, and what did he say? He testified against my grandpa."

"He told the truth."

Evan shrugged. "All's well that ends well. On the way home he said he'll take us fishing again and build the boat."

He started walking away from Buddy Jensen's house, saying over his shoulder, "Also, he told me about being shanghaied."

"What does that mean?" Buddy shouted.

"Ask him."

Supper that night went smoothly, and Evan noticed that his father no longer addressed Tom as "Pentreath." He was now "Tom," a new and respected friend. It was obvious that his father was enjoying the attention now being paid Evander Bryant Shoes and the family in general. He asked Tom if he'd pose with him outside the store. With Mr. Faircloth deceased, the Bryants were now the best known family on Hoople Street.

Having gotten the stories of Ozzie O'Brien and the *Hartlepool* and Dartmoor Prison off his chest, Grandfather Pentreath seemed like a new person. His eyes were brighter, and the monkey face smiled often, and there was a nice spring to his walk.

Next morning, they were in the barn rigging up Mike Hodge's stuffed pants legs. Evan was up on a stepladder, Tom instructing him how to tie off a halter hitch. "Loop it over the rafter, then bring the end of the line down and double it back — that's right — now it goes down. Pull it tight. There, you've done it."

Tom ran his end through the grommets, tying off, and Mike Hodge's pants dangled about four inches off the straw-strewn barn floor.

Tom stepped away and said, "Perfect. Get down and start to practice. Remember, fifteen minutes a day until school starts."

Evan put the ladder away and aimed his bad foot at Mike's crotch, missing. Too low. Then he missed again and fell down.

Tom winced and walked outside with the handsaw. Sooner or later the boy would target the red circle. Meanwhile, he thought his presence would make Evander nervous, frustrate him.

His daughter had told him that Howard wouldn't "dare" cut the practice pants down. She seemed to have gained confidence in the few days since he'd arrived and was willing to confront her husband. Hopefully, Tom at least had made that contribution. She was such a fine lady, and he wished Molly was still alive so he could thank her for that fact.

Buddy Jensen soon arrived and sat with Evan on the grass while Tom made the first carpenter's yellow marks on the inch and a half oak plank. "Here's where it all starts, the keel. All the strength of the boat begins right here."

Buddy said, "You don't bend it?"

"The keel is always flat, numskull," Evan said, gaining confidence himself.

"Not on a canoe like we have," Buddy said.

"This isn't a canoe," Evan said.

"I want to know what 'shanghaied' is, Mr. Pentreath," said Buddy.

As he started to draw the handsaw across the yellow mark at ten feet, one-half inch, Tom told Buddy about Miss Puckett's "crimp gang" kidnapping and added other details of the Barbary Coast like ponies that had their hoofs polished at bootblack stands, and Dab, the horse thief, and Hell Haggerty's African goat, Noobie, that ate caviar.

Tom gave them something to do:

"Get me the saw."

"Sand that joint."

"Get me that clamp."

When Tom went into the house to go to the bathroom, Evan said, "There's not another grandpa on earth like him."

Buddy said, "I think you're right."

18

" **A** H, the Moluccas, the ancient isles of Spice, in the Celebes Sea, surrounded by the Philippines and Borneo and New Guinea. What good memories I have of them — South from Ternate and Batjan, to Amboina and east to Banda's nutmeg groves. Here was the equator. I was on the barkentine *Rakati,* which means 'crab' in Malaysian. We were hauling spices to Hong Kong."

Tom paused in the midst of cutting oak for the stern of the boat, nodding to himself, recalling the East Indies.

Evan thought: You have to stay here until school starts so I can take you to Miss Wendy Appleton's geography class. She's probably never heard of any of those places.

"Two volcanoes framed a narrow passage between Ternate and Tidore the morning the *Rakati* sailed through, with the sun bursting over a storm cloud, letting us see the steep slopes of the islands, covered with jungle. Ternate has a great brown gash where the volcano sent molten lava down to the sea. It has thousands of green parrots in trees and lizards on the ground."

He just has to stay until school starts, Evan decided. Green parrots and lizards, imagine him saying that in front of the class, maybe using a pointer so that everyone could tell where the Celebes Sea was.

Jane Bryant was sitting nearby.

"We went to Ceram with its tree-climbing fish and millions of yellow butterflies one trip. Walking down a path by a stream I heard a crocodile splash and hurried away to harder ground. Ceram had cloves. We went to the small and most beautiful group, the Bandas, out toward New Guinea, for nutmeg. Unlike the palm trees, nutmeg must grow within the sound of the sea. We went to Boeroe for pepper and cajeput oil, from the cajeput tree. It's magic. You drink it, lather it over your body. It cures everything."

Evan wondered if it cured clubfoot.

"Did you see the crocodile?" Buddy Jensen asked.

"No, I didn't want to see it."

"Did England own all those islands?" Evan asked.

"No, the Dutch and Portuguese had them before I was born."

"No wonder you want to be a sailor, Evan," his mother said.

"Me, too," Buddy Jensen said. "Were there pirates out there?"

"Oh, yes, Chinese and Filipino and every other no-good scurvy sailor from Sumatra to Luzon. We had a cannon on the stern of the *Rakati* to fight with."

Oh, Lord, this could last all summer, Evan hoped.

His mother said, "Help me up. I'll go in and make some lemonade." She'd come outside to observe the boat building.

"Alas, the spice trade is now in Zanzibar, Pemba, and Madagascar."

"Last night you told me about a place where wives were traded for pigs," Evan said. He was trying to make Buddy Jensen jealous. Buddy was beside himself, ready to spend all day and all night at the Bryants'.

"The island of Nias, below Simalger in the Indian Ocean, off Sumatra. Pigs are used like money, and thousands of their jaws hang from the chief's palaces. Steal a pig and you die. Gold is everywhere, but no one knows how it got there. Boys your age wear tigertooth amulets on the sheaths of their fighting knives."

Buddy Jensen was about to go out of his head.

19

T H E boat was finished in five days, the work of a
master craftsman, caulked between the planking, put
together carefully with brass screws, receiving an un-
dercoat of white lead paint; ready for two finish coats
to be applied.

It was handsome, and Tom was quite pleased with
himself. Evan acted as if he'd just been given a new
Stutz. He kept saying, "It's beautiful, it's beautiful."
Including the oars and anchor, the final cost was
$27.30, at least $50 beneath the market price. Tom
was proud of himself.

Tom had asked Evan what he was going to name
his new boat. Evan said it was a surprise, and Tom

was pleased again when he saw Evan painting CHIPS on the stern and the bow in black letters.

Then he made a cart out of a pair of big pulley wheels from the junkyard down at Pinner's Point, and *Chips* was launched properly. Mrs. Jensen provided a small bottle of champagne to break over the prow. The ceremony was attended by Evan's mother and Buddy's mother and his father and Tom, but not Howard Bryant. He did not approve of alcoholic beverages.

Chips leaked a little after launching, but Tom assured Evan that as soon as the oakum caulking and planking swelled from water contact, the leaks would stop.

The inaugural fishing trip on the western branch of the Elizabeth River was scheduled for the next day, and Tom warned the boys that they'd have to do all the rowing. He did not say why beyond telling them that they'd have to learn how. It was simple, he said. *The last thing they needed was for his heart to act up.*

While Tom sat on the stern seat, the boys had some problems coordinating, but the tide was going out, and after a quarter mile they pulled together. Tom enjoyed himself, doing absolutely nothing.

Chips was soon anchored at the mouth of the river, and lines went overboard. This was croaker water, and Buddy Jensen caught the first one in midmorning.

Tom couldn't remember being so relaxed and peaceful in all his life. He'd accomplished what his grandson had asked for when his letter arrived at the International Seaman's Last Home; he was finally enjoying the love of his daughter, and the respect of her husband. After all the turmoil of those bad years, life couldn't be better.

Buddy Jensen said, "Grandpa," as if he, too, owned Thomas Pentreath, "tell us about prison, that one in England that the paper talked about last week."

Why not? Tom thought. They both should know what it was like in Dartmoor. Maybe it might make them think again if they ever decided to commit a crime. Unlikely but perhaps possible. One could never know exactly where the years could lead. One should be prepared.

So he talked about terrible Dartmoor and the beatings he received; the near-starvation; the icy, damp

cold of winter; the cruel warders and the pigeons who
kept him alive. That would warn them to behave.

The fishing was slow and wouldn't begin again un-
til the tide started in. He watched their young faces as
he talked — the wide frowns, the open mouths, the
disbelief that boys their age were held and tortured in
Dartmoor.

They had no questions, and he knew that they'd re-
member this time on the muddy Elizabeth for as long
as they lived.

Then Evan said, "Tell us about being shipwrecked
in the Java Sea," as if to try to erase Dartmoor.

"All right. The Java Sea is below Borneo. Now
that's a fascinating place I've never been. Anyhow,
we were proceeding south to Surabaya when the
Rakati ran into a freshening gale. I can remember
that her weather shrouds hummed under the pressure
of the wind. Back then, many of the reefs and shoals
weren't marked. We were about thirty miles from
port. Suddenly there was a big crash, and I heard
someone yell. 'Rudder's gone . . .'"

"What happened?" Evan asked.

"We'd skidded over a shoal, taking out some of the

bottom and ripping the rudder off its gudgeons. A ship is helpless without a rudder. We waded hip-deep to set up topping lifts and cast off halyards, not knowing how much hull we had left. She already had a list to leeward. She staggered and rolled drunkenly in the spray-filled darkness, and then the captain shouted, 'Abandon ship!' The problem with that was sharks."

"What did you do then?" Buddy Jensen asked, his eyes as big as goblets.

"Saw that the rudder was floating about twenty yards behind the ship when lightning flashed, and I dove overboard. Another bloke and myself sat on it all night. We were picked up just after dawn by a fishing boat. We cheated the sharks."

A little later, Tom, having missed his nap, dozed off. When he was half-awake again, he heard Buddy Jensen say, "I think I'm going into the coast guard."

Evan said, "I'd do that, too, if I didn't have this stupid foot."

20

D<small>URING</small> *the night, Tom awakened with chest pains and chewed a nitro pill. He didn't know what had brought the jolts on, but they'd happened occasionally in New York over the past year. They just happened. It was nearing time to go.*

The merchant marine hospital doctor had said, "Mr. Pentreath, your heart is getting old just like the rest of your body." Aye!

In the morning Tom asked, "How are you doing with Mike Hodge?"

Evan said, "Not very well."

"Show me."

They went out to the barn, Woody trotting behind, and Evan's kick landed on "Mike Hodge's" left knee.

"I missed again," he said despondently.

Tom said, "You have to aim higher and to the right. Plant your left foot, then swing the right foot. Let me show you."

"You've done this before?"

"A few times. Watch me." *That bar in Jayapura; the dock in Port Moresby.*

Tom connected with the red circle three times in a row, amazed at how spry he still was.

"Don't be discouraged. Just keep practicing. Let's go sit in the boat for a few minutes. We have to talk."

Evan followed him and climbed in, taking the stern seat so they were facing each other. Woody hopped in with them.

"Evander, I have to go back to Brooklyn."

Tears pooled, and Evan cried out, urgently, "No, you can't go. You have to stay here at least until school starts! You can't go!"

Tom was touched by the boy's reaction. It made him feel special once again.

"Evander, the baby is due the end of the week,

maybe sooner, and your mother doesn't need me around. The other thing is that I'll lose my room and bed at the rest home if I stay away longer than two weeks." He'd been away now for eleven days.

"Why can't you just stay with us forever?"

"Because it wouldn't be fair to your mother and father. I don't want them taking care of me as I grow older."

Several times during the visit, Tom had thought of Captain Scowcroft's dire prediction that he'd never return from his daughter's home. He would show the crusty old sailor that he was wrong. Leave now.

"Evander, who's to say that I won't come back, and we can go fishing together?" That was a true wish.

"Grandpa, please do that. Please come back."

Tom said, "And I'll start saving my money to pay your train fare to New York. I can show you around." *Give him hope, Tom thought. Perhaps it could happen if they didn't wait too long.*

"Will you write to me, Grandpa?"

"Of course, I will. I promise."

One last try. "But you have to go?"

"Yes, Evander, I have to go. I told your mother and father at breakfast."

"What did they say?"

"They said they understood."

Evan sighed sadly and deeply. "One last thing, can you teach me how to be a buzz saw? A wasp?"

Tom replied, "Of course."

A little later, Evan walked over to Buddy Jensen's house and said, "He's leaving."

Buddy said, "He can't do that."

"Yes, he can."

"Why?"

"He'll lose his room and bed in that rest home if he doesn't go back. Also, the baby is coming any day now."

"What does the baby have to do with him leaving?"

"He said my mother couldn't take care of him and the baby, but he'll come back to fish maybe, and I'll go to New York to see him there."

Buddy said, in a hopeless voice, "Take me along."

They sat in silence on the front porch for a few minutes, then Evan said, "Maybe there's a rest home for old sailors in Norfolk? That way, we can visit him, and he can come over here to visit us." Evan knew that Norfolk was one of the biggest seaports on the East Coast.

"Fish with us," Buddy cried jubilantly.

Silence again, then Evan said, "Should we tell him, or should we just go to Norfolk and find out for ourselves? Then surprise him."

"Just go ourselves. If we tell him he might say no. Do you have any money?"

"I can rob my piggy bank. All we need is streetcar and ferry money. Twenty cents each."

They caught the sidewheeler *Rockaway* in early afternoon to cross the Elizabeth and land at the foot of Commercial Street. This wasn't the first time they'd gone to Norfolk without permission and wouldn't be the last. Prowling the docks and looking at ships loading and unloading was relief from the prior dullness of Hoople Street. Now, it could boast a murder.

They walked up Commercial looking for a policeman but didn't find one until the corner of East Main, a street with a bad reputation for drinking and fighting of "tars," a nickname for sailors.

"I've never heard of a rest home for them, but there is a merchant marine hospital run by the government." The policeman gave them directions.

Evan asked the lady at the desk if she knew where there was a rest home for old sailors. "My grandpa needs one here."

"I've been asked about that before. There aren't any in Norfolk. If he's ill, he can come here free of charge."

"He walks with a cane, but he's not sick."

"We can't help you. I'm sorry."

They went outside and sat on the stone steps, dejected.

Buddy said, "Well, we tried. Do you want to go down and watch some ships?"

Evan nodded. "I'll tell him tonight."

When Tom went up to bed that night there was a sheet of school paper on his pillow. The penciled message said: *Grandpa, Thank you for everything, especially my boat. I love your stories. Please come back soon. I love you. Evander.*

21

SEABOARD Coast Line engine Number 16 was breathing heavily, steam escaping from the huge pistons, smoke curling out of its stack, ready to roll north for Richmond and Washington with its seven dark green passenger cars.

Evan, his parents, and Buddy Jensen were on the platform along with Tom. Even Howard had taken time off from selling shoes to walk down to the end of High Street.

He said, "Well, Tom, you've changed us all for good. I'm so glad you came."

Tom replied, "It's been a wonderful visit, Howard. Have a good baby, Jane, girl or boy."

Close to tears, she said, "I promise you'll know. Whichever sex, the middle name will be Chips."

Buddy Jensen threw his arms around Tom's neck and said good-bye.

Both Evan and Buddy Jensen were leaking tears, and Tom put his shoulder next to Evan. "Walk with me a little ways."

The old man and the boy limped off down the platform. "Evander, I want you to become a surgeon, not a sailor. I want you to help other boys and girls who have a bad foot."

Evan nodded. He couldn't speak. His jaws were locked in grief. He stopped and threw his arms around Tom, nodding again.

The conductor shouted the inevitable, "All aboard," and Tom picked up his seabag, and they all moved to the steps of Car 4. Tom mounted them, turned and waved, and disappeared inside.

Moments later, Engine 16 backed out, bell ringing, whistle blowing to make the turnaround and thunder away.

Molly Chips Bryant was born a week later. In time, she would be told all about her grandpa.

––––––

In late August, Jane received a letter from Brooklyn.

My dear Mrs. Bryant:

I regret to inform you that your father, Thomas Pentreath, passed away peacefully in bed last night. A shipmate of mine, he was a man of good character and integrity despite youthful occurrences.

When he returned here he often talked about you and your family, especially Evander and his friend Buddy Jensen. His visit was plainly the highlight of his life.

He wrote a one-page will leaving his eternal love for his only family and an Excelsior fountain pen for Evander. I shall send both. His only other possessions were a seabag and the clothes on his back.

In accordance with his wishes, tomorrow I will employ the steam tug Mary Moran *and take him out beyond the Ambrose Lightship and commit his body to the deep with the following traditional seaman's burial prayer:*

To Thee, O Lord, we commend the soul of Thy servant, Thomas Pentreath, that having departed from this world he may live with Thee; and whatever sins he has committed through the frailty of human nature, do Thou, in Thy most tender mercy, forgive and wash away. Through Christ, Our Lord. Amen.

Percival Scowcroft
Master Mariner

IN September, on the first day of school, Mike Hodge stopped Evan in the hallway and took away his lunch bag. "Let's see what's in here."

Evan took aim and hit Mike Hodge you-know-where with his clubfoot.

Mike screamed in pain and dropped to his knees, clutching himself.

Evan lifted his head toward heaven and smiled, then leaned down to say, "I'd rather be your friend, but if you want to fight I'll turn into a buzz saw."

Grandpa Chips Pentreath would have liked that, Evan thought.

Literature Circle Questions

Use the questions and activities that follow to get more out of the experience of reading *A Sailor Returns* by Theodore Taylor.

KNOWLEDGE

1. Before Evan meets his grandfather, he tells his friend, Buddy, some things about his grandfather. What are three things Evan tells Buddy that are not true?

2. Evan's grandfather doesn't tell Evan or Evan's mother that he isn't well. Find three passages in the story that show he is ill.

3. On page 71, there are some clues to let us know what year the story takes place. What year is it?

COMPREHENSION

4. In school, Evan often gets picked on by Mike Hodge. Explain why Evan is such an easy target for a bully.

5. At the beginning of the story, Evan's father is rude to Tom Pentreath. Describe the events that lead to a change in this relationship.

6. Before Evan meets his grandfather, he imagines that he is a giant, strong man. What are some ways that Evan and his grandfather are alike? Why are these similarities important to Evan?

APPLICATION

7. During the story we see Evan's mother go through some changes. What evidence can you find to show these changes?

8. Evan's father refers to him as a cripple. Find three passages that demonstrate how Evan is able to stand up to physical challenges.

ANALYSIS

9. When Evan's grandfather finds out that Mike Hodge is bullying Evan, he gives Evan advice. What advice does he give? Compare this to the advice that Evan's father might give.

Note: The following questions are keyed to Bloom's taxonomy as follows: Knowledge: 1-3; Comprehension: 4-6; Application: 7, 8; Analysis: 9, 10; Synthesis: 11, 12; Evaluation: 13, 14.

10. Evan and his grandfather learn a lot from each other. Give two specific examples of how Evan and his grandfather have changed by the end of the novel.

SYNTHESIS

11. Propose an alternate solution to dealing with Mike Hodge to the one Evan's grandfather offers.

12. Evan's grandfather is not a big man. He tells many stories about being a young man at sea. Many of these stories show him having to prove himself. Find examples of how Evan's grandfather is still trying to prove himself.

EVALUATION

13. Evan's mother forgives her father (Evan's grandfather) for leaving when she was only three years old. Defend her father's actions based on what we find out in the story.

14. Why did Evan's grandfather choose to go back to his retirement home in Brooklyn at the end of the story?

ACTIVITIES

1. Evan's grandfather tells him many stories about his sea adventures. Pick one place where Evan's grandfather traveled. Find it on a map. Using magazines and the Internet, create a collage about the place you chose. On a 5" x 7" index card, write a paragraph with important information, such as who lives there, what country it is part of, and what natural resources can be found there. Share your findings with a classmate.

2. Evan's grandfather gets put in prison for killing a man even though he was defending himself. Should he have gone to prison? Host a trial in your classroom. Decide who will be Thomas Pentreath, his lawyer, the jury, and the judge. You might even have witnesses. (Remember, our laws are probably different than the laws of 19th Century England.)

3. Thomas Pentreath was a sailor in the 1800s. Pair up with another student and find out about sailing ships. Are they still used? What are they used for? What are the various duties people have on sailing ships? Interview someone from the Coast Guard, go on-line to find information about ships, or go to your library and get books about sailing and ships.